ONE NIGHT WITH
HER BROODING
BODYGUARD

ONE NIGHT WITH HER BROODING BODYGUARD

CARA COLTER

MILLS & BOON

First published in Great Britain 2020
by Mills & Boon, an imprint of HarperCollins*Publishers*
1 London Bridge Street, London, SE1 9GF

Large Print edition 2021

ISBN: 978-0-263-28981-7

MIX
Paper from
responsible sources
FSC® C007454

This book is produced from independently certified FSC™ paper to ensure responsible forest management. For more information visit www.harpercollins.co.uk/green.

Printed and bound in Great Britain
by CPI Group (UK) Ltd, Croydon, CR0 4YY

With deep gratitude for the power, beauty and mystery of sisterhood.

Avon. Collette. Anna.

Forever joined.

PROLOGUE

"LANCASTER, I'VE RARELY seen *that* look on your face."

It reminded Connal Lancaster that Prince Edward Alexander of Havenhurst was one of the few people who could truly read him.

Though Edward and Lancaster were more like brothers than a prince and his protector, few people, including the prince, ever addressed Lancaster by either his rank, which was major, or his first name. Prince Edward had never used it, not even when they had traveled incognito to Mountain Bend, Oregon, four years ago.

The trip that had changed everything and brought the island kingdom of Havenhurst their beloved princess.

"What look, sir?" Lancaster asked, comfortable with formality between them despite the closeness of their relationship.

"Fear," Prince Edward said, after a moment's consideration. "Make that I've *never* seen that look on your face. You said you had to see me on an urgent security matter this morning."

Lancaster, ever the warrior, felt insulted by the use of that particular word to describe anything about himself.

"Not fear, Your Highness," he said, firmly, and then after just a moment's hesitation, "but certainly apprehension."

"All right," the prince conceded, "apprehension. It reminds me of that time in Mountain Bend when I was recognized at the Ritz concert. Something battle-ready about you. What's going on?" He gestured at the chair in front of his desk, and Lancaster took it.

"I had a call from Interpol this morning," Lancaster said, without preamble. "A very concerning call. A shadowy group has appeared on their radar. They've intercepted threads of some disturbing internet chatter. It involves Havenhurst."

"A threat to Havenhurst?" Prince Edward asked, and a ripple of shock crossed his face. Havenhurst was little more than a speck in the North Atlantic, two hundred kilometers from the North Channel. Except for ancient scuffles with nearby islands, there had never been a risk to the kingdom. "A danger worthy of a warning from an international police organization?"

The prince's marriage to Madeline Nelson, an ordinary American woman, had brought an abundance of publicity to the Havenhurst, relatively unknown to the world before that. The birth of their son, Prince Ryan Lancaster—named, to Lancaster's great pride, after both Maddie's father and himself—had cemented the royal couple's celebrity status.

Now, with Maddie pregnant with the second royal baby, Lancaster was uncomfortably aware of the whole world watching them endlessly and obsessively. That obsession made his job more difficult, though he certainly recognized the celebrity was both a gift and an annoyance. The gift was that it had benefited the economies in both Maddie's home town of Mountain Bend, Oregon, and this small island nation. The newfound fame meant both places could barely keep up with the demand for their exports, and that tourism had exploded.

The annoyance was the cameras, the media attention, the stories and articles—sometimes true, sometimes false—were constant intrusions on the family's privacy. For Lancaster, it had created a need to come up with increasingly complex ways of shielding the royal family from a celebrity-besotted world.

For the most part Lancaster, unflappable, took the new complexity of his duty to protect Edward and his family in stride.

Until now.

After Edward's mention of the word *fear*, he had stripped his features of emotion. He was pretty sure he looked, as always, as if his expression had been cast in stone, and gave away nothing. And yet he had to admit, despite his denial, there was some uncomfortable truth to the prince's observation.

But then Edward had known Lancaster since they both were children. He would read what others would not: the brows lowered, the downturn of the mouth, the hand resting a little too close to the hilt on his belt. All spoke an unusual tension—apprehension—in a man who took extraordinary pride in his ability to remain calm.

Lancaster took pride, too, in the fact that Edward and his family felt so safe precisely because Lancaster never did. No matter how peaceful the island might seem, he never let down his guard, never stopped training, never stopped watching, never relaxed his attitude toward his responsibilities to the royal family.

"It's not precisely a threat to Havenhurst," Lancaster said, his tone deliberately measured. "What's come to the attention of Interpol is what appears to be a series of kidnapping plots."

"Kidnapping? Ryan?" Edward asked, his tone strangled, his understanding of the apprehension he had seen in Lancaster's face suddenly solidified.

Lancaster gave him a dark look that assured him of the safety of his family. He would lay down his life to protect them, and an enemy would never meet a more formidable opponent.

"There is no direct threat to any member of your family, Your Highness," Lancaster said. "That is the diabolic brilliance of these plots that are unfolding. Whoever is perpetrating them knows they can't go after an actual member of a royal family, a high-profile politician, a famous musician or movie star. These people are too well protected.

"What came to Interpol's attention were fragments of a list. It had a dozen names on it of very prominent people, in a code, which they broke. At first they could make no sense of it. Because it would have a target's name in code—for example, Henry Hampton—" he named a famous concert pianist who had been recently knighted by the British queen "—and then a name appearing beside that name, not in code, that no one had ever heard of.

"But good police work unveiled this—those unheard of people have strong ties to the rich and famous. They are childhood friends, or a favorite aunt or uncle, trusted confidants, sometimes secret lovers, people who are close but well outside the circle of protection."

"Who?" Edward asked.

"It was Princess Madeline's name that was decoded."

Edward blanched. "Who have they targeted in her circle?"

Frowning, Lancaster handed him a folded piece of paper.

Edward unfolded it, and saw it had written on it a single name.

Sophie Kettle

"Sophie," Edward said, softly. "Maddie's best friend. Godmother to Ryan." His eyes went to Lancaster and the rest of what Sophie was in their shared history remained unspoken between the two men.

Lancaster cleared his throat. "She's very much on the loose around the world since she does PR for that rock band, the Ritz. Sophie Kettle would make an unfortunately easy target."

"She was fired last week."

Something flickered in Lancaster, uncomfortable and alien. That very thing he claimed never to feel? Fear? "Which probably makes her an even easier target."

"I can't tell Maddie this. She's just been so unwell. I can't add an additional stress right now."

The prince's great love for his wife—and how appalled he was at the idea of keeping a secret from her—was evident in his face. Lancaster quickly quelled the sharp awareness of his own solitary existence that the prince's devotion to Maddie created in him.

"Agreed. It would be best not to share the details with the princess. And not with Miss Kettle, either. You know her. She will decide she doesn't need protection, at all."

"Unless we made it clear that you were to be her protector," Edward said, a slight teasing note to his voice.

"She's engaged," Lancaster said, his tone flat, making his eyes hard with a warning that there were places even a prince should fear to go.

"Apparently she's not that anymore, either."

This was news to Lancaster, and he was not sure what dangerous emotion tickled along his spine, though he made sure his expression did not reveal it, and he refused to ask the question *When did that happen?* He got back to his point.

"I've got someone en route to keeping an eye on Sophie. If we can get her to Havenhurst, we can contain the situation. The fact that she's just lost her job—and her engagement—plays straight into our hands. So does Princess Madeline's having a difficult pregnancy—sorry, sir, the palace staff has been talking about rather epic bouts of morning sickness, and Prince Ryan is being particularly fractious of late."

"A holy terror," Prince Edward agreed, wearily. "His nanny tells me it is quite normal for a two-year-old, but it's being exacerbated by his mother not having her usual amount of energy and time for him, I'm sure."

"Wouldn't it be the most natural time in the world for Maddie to ask her friend to come and support her?" Lancaster suggested softly. "Sophie is excellent with the prince."

"You've thought this out," Edward said gratefully. "It *would* be the perfect time for Sophie to come for an extended visit. I will go plant the seed."

"If you can insert a sense of urgency, sir—"

"Understood," Edward said.

"Your Highness?"

"Yes?"

"If either of these two women were ever to find out we've left them out of the loop on this thing, even though it is for their own good, I'm afraid it won't go well for us."

"You've always had a gift for the understatement, Lancaster."

And then both men enjoyed a quiet, comradely chuckle born of the intricacies of dealing with strong-willed American women in delicate situations.

CHAPTER ONE

THUNK.

Sophie Kettle gripped the deep leather armrests of her seat. Logically, she knew she had just heard the engagement of the landing gear on the private royal jet she was a passenger on. But it felt more as if she had heard the sound of her own heart falling.

Nonsense, she told herself, firmly. She was a freshly scorned woman. Her heart, what was left of it, was curled up in a protective little ball, behind the walls of a newly buttressed fortress. It was certainly not *falling*.

And yet when Maddie had said, *"Lancaster will meet you,"* why had Sophie wanted to protest? And strenuously?

She had wanted to ask Maddie to send someone—anyone—else. But that would have been like broadcasting that her feelings for Lancaster—her recent heartbreak not acting as any kind of cautionary tale—were the very same as her feelings for him had always been. As soon as Maddie had mentioned his name, Sophie's emotions had started dancing just out of the range of her control, like a high-strung Pomeranian refusing to be caught. Or tamed.

"Your feelings are like a badly behaved Pomeranian?" she scoffed at herself. It was a measure, really, of what bad shape she was in.

As she gazed out the window, the plane began its descent, and the island of Havenhurst came into view. It wasn't the first time she had been here, but this time it seemed different. The lush forests, the rolling hills, the green fields, the village, the castle, it all felt altered because, this time, this place was going to be home for as long as Maddie needed her.

And really, it couldn't have come at a better time. Except for—the jet landed with a gentle tap, and coasted down the runway—him.

Out the oval of her window, Sophie saw Lancaster, as the plane glided to a complete halt. There was the *thunk* again, no landing gear to blame it on this time.

He was on the tarmac, standing in front of a black, sleek car that flew the royal flags on each side of it. He was wearing his everyday uniform, his beret tucked under the epaulet on the shoulder.

As ordinary as it was, that knife-pressed uniform, the alert calm in the way he held himself, made Lancaster look exactly like what he was: a warrior, and a Celtic warrior at that. Tall, strong, fit…ready, somehow, for the things regular people were not ready for.

A whisper of a breeze drew Sophie's eyes to his hair. It was the beautiful red-gold of fall leaves and longer than she had seen it before. As she watched, the breeze teased it slightly, lifting strands off the wideness of his brow.

Really, Sophie chided herself, he was just an ordinary man, in a drab green working uniform. It wasn't even the resplendent dress uniform—goodness, that man could rock a kilt—she had seen him in at Prince Ryan's christening, where he had been godfather and she had been godmother.

Not that she wanted to think about that event. Ever again. The godmother/godfather thing had made her feel unrealistically connected to Lancaster. At the reception, after just a touch too much wine—

Good grief! It was two years ago. Was she still embarrassed?

Yes.

As Lancaster lifted his eyes to the plane, scanning the windows, Sophie felt herself sinking down in her seat. She did not want him to catch her watching him! He might surmise she was studying him, unchanged from the obsessive teenager she had been the first time she had seen him.

She did not want him to know, ever, that what she felt right now, catching that first glimpse of him again, was the same thing she had felt when she was that teenager and he walked through the doors of the Black Kettle Café in Mountain Bend, Oregon, four years ago.

So much life had happened to her since then!

And yet, there it was. Her eyes had touched on him, and it felt as if her heart was falling, as if all the world was fading, until her vision became a dark tunnel that ended in the bright light that was him.

Lancaster.

She slid back up a bit, squinted at him and slid back down. Rationally, he did not look like any kind of a bright light!

His handsome, perfectly sculpted features were closed, and if anything, when he gazed directly at her window, having seen her despite her efforts to shrink away, something around the line of that sensual mouth tightened marginally.

Well, who could blame him? She'd been just barely an adult—fresh out of high school—the first time she had met him. She could feel her cheeks burn, even now, as she recalled chasing him so shamelessly, his firm putting away of her, as if he saw only the child she had wanted so desperately to outgrow.

Two years later, at the christening, she had been even more intent on proving to him she was a grown-up in every way that was possible. Even without the excuse of her youth, he had rejected her. Rather resoundingly!

Lancaster was an attractive man. Feeling attracted to him *was* natural, a function of biology, nothing more.

Well, since then, Sophie had matured. Come into herself. Men chased her, not the other way around. Her fiancé—now ex-fiancé, Troy—had been relentless in declaring his love.

So why had it all fallen apart?

Sophie shook it off. The point wasn't that her

relationship had failed, but that she was more jaundiced about true love, now. Romance was for children, and she had long since lost her childhood.

This time it would be different around Lancaster, she told herself, because she had the tools of disillusionment to override her sense of being pulled toward him like a magnet being pulled to steel.

Taking a breath, Sophie pulled herself back up, forced herself to look out the window, and straight at him.

His eyes met hers through the plane window. His eyes were a cool color of jade that she had never seen in another human being. In her weakest moments, she had wondered if he would pass that feature on to his children.

In her weaker than weakest moments, she had wondered what the combination of her blue eyes and his green eyes—

Thunk.

Biology, Sophie reminded herself firmly. She was a lucky woman, indeed. The universe had brought her this opportunity to test her newly hardened philosophies on men, romance, life and the value of total independence for women.

She broke eye contact with him—she did not smile at him, because he did not smile at her—and got up from her seat, gathering her things.

She took one final glance down at herself and congratulated herself that this part, the image she was projecting, was just right.

At the christening, she had been so eager to overcome that waitress-in-a-small-town first impression she had made on Lancaster that she had worn a gown. It had been a confection of gray mist and pure sexiness. It had been her first designer purchase. It had seemed to reflect the new sophisticated her, a college graduate now, ready to take on the world with her freshly minted two-year marketing diploma.

Or marry Lancaster, if he had asked.

In retrospect the gown had been way too sexy for the occasion, though the brief light that had come on in Lancaster's eyes, when he had gazed at her over the head of the godson he held in his arms, had made it worth the investment.

That look, as it turned out, had been his one moment of weakness in the whole disastrous weekend.

Sophie, she told herself firmly, *you are not taking that particular walk down memory lane.*

Today, Sophie considered herself way more a jaded woman of the world—broken engagement under her belt, world travels because of her job with the band—and her outfit reflected that. She was dressed casually in narrow stretch jeans that showed off the length and slenderness of her legs.

She had paired the jeans with a white button-down shirt that she had unbuttoned quite a ways down. She had on a white tank underneath it, and had belted the shirt. The outfit was saved from total "photographer on safari" by a pair of stilettos that stretched her five foot six to an easy five foot nine.

Her long black hair was loose and straight, and she knew from experience that that particular look was a total temptation to men. Still, the last thing she wanted was for Lancaster to think she was trying to tempt him—*again*—a horrible little voice inside her insisted on reminding her. So, just before she picked up her oversize handbag, she scooped her hair back into a clip, and dabbed on a bit of clear lip gloss.

She wished she had a mirror that would confirm she had accomplished the *I'm just not that into you* look that she aspired to.

A crew member opened the door of the private jet, and she passed the captain and crew to get to the door. She thanked them for the flight, aware that inside she was still the small-town girl who, despite life experiences, sometimes looked at her circumstances and wanted to pinch herself.

Here she was, Sophie Kettle, arriving at the castle of her good friends, who were royalty. She was the godmother to a prince!

She stepped out of the plane and made herself pause and take a deep breath. She felt the warmth of sunshine on her face, drank in the crisp scents of fall that were in the air. Then, she allowed herself to look at him.

Lancaster had moved to the bottom of the stairs. His expression was bland, an annoyingly professional mask in place, ready to do his duty and assist her if need be.

Not knowing that she would not accept assistance from him if he was the last man in the universe.

Which was, of course, precisely the kind of vow the universe liked to play havoc with.

Because, as she descended the narrow gangway, on the third step from the tarmac, her oversize bag caught on a metal rivet in the handrail.

It stopped her forward momentum with shocking abruptness, and the high heels proved ridiculous when faced with the obstacle of unexpectedly being thrown off balance.

She lurched forward, and probably would have fallen down the remaining few steps and crashed into the asphalt.

Except for Lancaster, who was always aggravatingly ready for anything, including, it seemed, a woman falling into his arms.

Sophie registered that he did not even have the decency to look startled as he moved gracefully up the narrow step and blocked her fall with his own body.

She hit him with enough force that it should have knocked them both over, but he was rock steady. His arms folded around her, absorbing some of her momentum. Still, she found her nose squished into the solid strength of his chest, her body crushed against the hard, uncompromising length of his.

Biology was definitely trumping her life experiences!

Because time stopped. She was enveloped in him. His scent was tangy and clean, so utterly masculine it made her feel a dizzy sense of longing. She could feel the strong, steady beat of his heart beneath the crisp fabric of his tunic, the play of warm skin and hard muscle beneath that.

A sensation welled up in her of pure and unadulterated longing, and something even more unsettling. Homecoming.

As if this was the only place she had ever wanted to be, in the circle of Lancaster's arms.

She crooked her neck and looked up at him.

He stared down at her.

She could see the faintest growth of red-gold stubble on his cheeks and chin, and she remembered the taste of his lips when she had stolen a kiss from them at the christening. She had to fight an insane desire to trace the firm fullness of his bottom one with her fingertip.

That would shatter his composure! That familiar electricity was thrumming dangerously in the air between them. Or, if their history was any indication, thrumming dangerously in her, and he was not feeling a thing.

His voice seemed to confirm the latter was true. She was on fire. He was on ice.

"Miss Kettle," he said, and his voice licked at that fire within her as if it had been fed oxygen. The brogue, the tone, the totally unconscious sexiness of it, made her want to stay crushed against him for as long as he would allow it.

"We meet again."

Even though she loved his voice, the faintly amused—or maybe it was annoyed—note penetrated. He said it as if she had *planned* to tumble into his arms.

Given her past indiscretions where he was concerned, that probably wasn't such a stretch, but it was still aggravating. And humiliating.

Her brain kicked in fully. Obviously, the *Miss Kettle* was setting up a deliberate barrier between them, and that was a good thing. She pushed hastily away, certain he had not indulged the long embrace out of affection.

He was too much of a gentleman to shove her away before he was certain she had achieved her balance. She teetered on the stair above him, cursing the shoes she had adored just minutes ago. Carefully, she straightened her clothing, anchored her bag firmly on her shoulder and moved down the remaining stairs, ignoring the hand he held out as he stepped back from her.

"Aren't you being ridiculously formal?" she asked, brushing by him. "We share a godson.

We love all the same people. We're practically family."

"But we're not family," he said, with elaborate patience as if she was being slightly trying, like a small child who needed help with table manners.

She paused and looked back over her shoulder at him. Was he ever going to stop seeing her as a child? It made her want to—her eyes skittered to that lip she had just wanted to touch with her fingertip—well, it made her want to do what she always wanted to do around him.

Which, she should not have to remind herself, had always led to humiliation and disaster.

Sophie reminded herself of the new her: hardened to romantic illusions of any sort, able to discern that following biological impulses, as strong as they might be, could not possibly lead to wise decisions.

"All right, then. Yes, we meet again, Mr. Lancaster," she returned, her voice chilly, her eyes deliberately moving away from his lips. She drew herself to her full shoe-enhanced height, and lifted her chin.

He cocked his head at her. "Lancaster is fine."

She turned to face him, full on. "If you're

going to call me *Miss* Kettle, I'm going to call you *Mr.* Lancaster."

"I didn't mean to offend you. You're not here as my acquaintance, but as a guest of the prince and princess. If you prefer me to call you by your first name, you can invite me to do so."

Oh! There was that temptation again! To shock that formality right out of him. But of course, it would just confirm, in his mind, that she was as immature as ever.

Was she as immature as ever?

"Can I call *you* by your first name?" she asked. She had always called him Lancaster, always used that name in her mind. The name had always seemed complete in itself. It even had a certain sensuous pull to it. Wouldn't it make a great start to their new chapter if he had a nice unassuming first name like Melvin or Dunstan or Felix?

"No one calls me by my given name," he said. A smile attempted to make that not quite as unfriendly as it was.

"I don't even know your first name," she realized.

"As I said, since I entered the guard, no one uses it, so it's not really necessary to know it."

"No one uses your fist name?" she said, skeptically.

"No."

"Not your mother?"

"My mother's gone."

Sophie had a sudden desire to ask him if his wife had called him by his first name. It was really the only personal detail about himself he had ever shared with her, that he was a widower who had lost his wife and young son to a fire. But casting a quick glance at his closed features, she sensed that would be crossing a line, going to the place no one ever went with him.

It made her aware of how alone he was in the world. And that the last thing he would ever appreciate was her thinking that needed fixing.

"Okay then, Mr. Lancaster," she said. "If no first name is forthcoming, you may call me Miss Kettle."

He regarded her thoughtfully for a moment. "It's Major, if you would prefer formalities." He said this so reasonably that she wanted to kick him. That should startle that impassive look off his face. She also fought the plain and childish urge to say *You started it*.

Instead, she narrowed her eyes at him, and flicked her hair.

"Whatever," she said, with what she could only hope was supreme indifference. Then on an impulse, she shrugged her bag off her shoulder and shoved it into his arms. He wanted to be treated like a servant? Fine! She put her nose even higher in the air, went to the car and opened the front passenger door, slid in and slammed it shut.

She smiled as she looked through the tinted glass at the flummoxed expression on his face as he gazed down at her bag.

"It's not going to be the way you expect, Mr. Lancaster," she promised him under her breath. "It's not going to be the way you expect, at all."

Of course, *then* she noticed that the steering wheel was on the right-hand side of the vehicle, the opposite of what it would have been back home in the United States. She had inadvertently gotten in the driver's side.

Sophie sighed, and had the awful thought that maybe it wasn't going to be the way *she* expected. At all.

CHAPTER TWO

LANCASTER LOOKED DOWN at the bag in his hands, bemused.

His first sensation, when Sophie had stepped out of that plane, had been one of abject relief. She was in his territory, now. He could keep her safe.

Of course, typical of Sophie, his comfortable sense of being in control had lasted less than a second. He had become aware, as she stood there in the doorway of the plane, how truly beautiful she was, more so even than the last time he had seen her. It was as if she was coming into herself in new—and dangerous—ways.

She had clipped back that waterfall of black hair, shiny as a fresh-tarred road, but it only made the exquisite bone structure of her face more apparent. Her eyes were as blue—and as changing—as the waters of the famous hot springs that dotted Havenhurst.

He hadn't seen her since Prince Ryan's christening. There had been opportunities. Princess Madeline had met Sophie in Mountain Bend several times to work on the town revitalization projects, but he had stepped back from the security team on those occasions.

From the christening, he remembered how young she was—twenty at the time—wearing that dress that had been way too grown up for her. The dress that actually made her look younger because it was so unsuitable, but it had telegraphed she was in that place where she was discovering her power as a woman, but still had to have too much to drink to be comfortable with that power. It was the too-much-to-drink part that had enabled him to put her off.

Though in truth, her lips had scorched like a permanent brand, and changed, probably for all time, the way he looked at her.

Which explained the avoidance strategy he had employed on all things Sophie Kettle to date.

Now, seeing her standing at the top of the steps coming down from the plane, he was aware that Sophie Kettle had come into herself, and that the transition was complete. There seemed to be no uncertainty left in the woman who came toward him.

She'd always been striking. Now, there was a layer of sophistication there that brought it to the next level.

The word *dangerous* came to his mind again. But he was a man who had prepared for danger all his life, and his strategy of avoiding her had worked well, so far, and would work again.

And then, fifteen seconds in—giving him fair warning nothing was going to go according to his plan where she was concerned—she had been in his arms. He had felt the soft crush of her body against his, looked into the sapphire of her eyes and breathed in the spring water freshness of her, and felt about as unsafe as he had ever felt.

Not just from her.

But from a longing that had bubbled to the surface in him. Had been bubbling, really, ever since Edward and Maddie had started showing him, on a daily basis, what it meant to share a life with another instead of going it alone.

Lancaster reminded himself, grimly, that he'd had that once. He had failed and he was not a man who tolerated failure—or would leave himself open to it again.

With that fresh resolve he watched, still bemused, as Sophie realized she had taken the driver's side of the vehicle. She got out, gave him a dirty look, as if it was somehow his fault she had ended up behind the steering wheel, and then got in the passenger door.

Still the front seat.

He deposited her bag in the back seat, took a deep breath, opened his door and slid in.

"I'd prefer if you rode in the back," he told her, his level tone not betraying, in the least, how essential it felt to get the barriers up between them and keep them there.

Her carefully clipped-back wave of shiny black hair had fallen over one shoulder, and she tossed it back. "I prefer riding in the front. And this time, your preferences don't override mine."

He cast her a look out of the corner of his eye, and saw from the delicate blush rising in her cheeks that she regretted saying that. She turned her face and looked out the window.

The last time it had been what he preferred, she had had a bit too much to drink at Ryan's christening. She'd wanted his lips. He had wanted hers, too, but luckily discipline was part of his daily routine, and he had managed to walk away from the temptations she offered. Sophie didn't ever need to know how hard that had been.

"The preference is not mine, exactly," he told her reasonably. "We have certain protocols. Guests of the prince and princess do not generally ride in the front seat. Nor do the staff address them by their first names."

She snorted. "There's no need to act as if you're the hired help."

From the woman who had just handed him her bag! He wasn't going to win this one, but he could take his victories where he could get them. Sophie was here. She was safe. If she was planning on being aggravating—and apparently she was—that was a small price to pay. He was going to have to pick his battles with her very carefully. And so he started the vehicle and put it in gear without saying what he wanted, which was that he *was* the hired help, and they'd both do well to remember that.

But, of course, it wasn't that simple, because she was right. They had a shared love of certain people that would make their lives forever more complicated and interwoven than he wanted them to be.

She apparently read his intention to ignore her,

and was having none of it. "Major, what's new in your life since we last met?"

"My life," he said, "is relatively unchanging." This fact was usually a comfort to him. Today, for a reason he did not care to explore, it felt different.

"Wild adventures?" she prodded him. "A great vacation, maybe? Learned to play the bagpipes? Jumped in some fall leaves? Have a girlfriend? Acquired a dog? Or a plant? Something that *needs* you?"

It bothered him more than he would ever let on that she had gone straight to his weakness. He had been needed once. It was not something he had taken to or wanted to experience again.

"My job needs me," he said.

"Uh-huh." She managed to utter that phrase with a total lack of conviction.

Lancaster realized that tucked in her seemingly casual questions, between breaths, was what she really wanted to know.

Lie, he ordered himself. This whole exercise was going to be so much simpler if she thought he had a girlfriend. But he found he could lie easily enough for her benefit—to get her to the safety of Havenhurst—but not so easily for his own.

"Nothing has changed much for me since the last time we met," he said.

"Ah. Unlike me. I've moved six times. Traveled the world with a band. Had a great job. Lost a great job. Been engaged. Then not engaged. It's been a whirlwind."

Her tone was light, layered with a new sophistication, as if she had breezed through the whirlwind life had thrown at her. He said nothing.

"I don't have the same illusions I once had," she said firmly, "romantic or otherwise."

He didn't say anything.

"I'm trying to reassure you, Major. I mean, I did have a crush on you at one time. Obviously. I don't anymore."

He wasn't sure if he was relieved or disconcerted that she intended to tackle their history head-on. Did he feel just a tiny twinge of *something* when she said that?

Yeah, like relief, Lancaster told himself sternly.

"I'm cynical, now. Off men. Nursing a wound, so to speak."

Out loud, he said, "I'm sorry you've had a rough go, Sophie."

"I thought you weren't going to call me by my first name." She had pulled that thick wave of hair back over her shoulder and was running it between her hands. He could smell the scent of her shampoo—light, clean, a hint of lemongrass.

"I thought so, too," he said. That was a reminder how hard it was going to be not to cross lines with her. He needed to be quiet, now. Drive her to the castle. Hand her over to Princess Madeline, and the security detail he had handpicked for her.

He told himself it was only because of his job that he needed to probe her mental state.

"It happened recently?" he asked.

"Last week." She tossed her head as if it didn't matter a whit. He wished she wouldn't do that.

"Still a fairly fresh wound, then."

"I'm not going to start crying, if that's what you're worried about."

He glanced at her. Despite her claim there were, indeed, tears sparking behind her eyes.

"Anyway, I was engaged to one of the security guys for the band. I seem to go for a type, don't I? Women found him completely irresistible."

Lancaster heard the sharp note of betrayal right under the flippant tone.

"Anyway, it was not a pretty split. I broke a guitar over his head. It was a Fender. I got fired, which was totally unfair, but then, who expects life to be fair?"

Lancaster slid her a glance again. He was not sure, but it seemed as if she might be more *mad* than *sad*. He was also not sure which would be easier to deal with.

Not, he reminded himself, that he would be dealing with it. She would not be happy to know he already knew what she had just told him, except for the part about women finding her fiancé irresistible. He'd been caught by surprise when the prince had told him she'd been fired, but he'd done his homework since then. She'd think it was intrusive, how much he now knew about her.

But that was his job. The more he knew about her, the better his chances of doing that job— keeping her safe, and by extension, the Royal Family.

"How old are you, Sophie?" Of course, he knew that, too.

"Twenty-two," she said, annoyed. He couldn't tell if she was annoyed that he had asked, or annoyed that he appeared to have forgotten, because they had shared this information before.

"That's very young to be making lifelong commitments." What was he doing? Trying to comfort her? Trying to tell her it was a good thing her engagement had ended? Or warning her not to jump from the fire into the frying pan? Particularly if, despite her denials, the frying pan was him?

"How old are you?" she asked him. "Thirty, now?"

He nodded. He refrained from saying, though he wanted to, *Way too old for you.*

"And how old were you when you got married?"

He hesitated. "Nineteen."

"Humph."

"It was different for me. Havenhurst is different. It's a more traditional kind of culture than the United States. People grow up faster here, marry younger. I had followed family tradition and joined the guard when I was seventeen, so I considered myself established at nineteen."

"Oh, and that wasn't a lifelong commitment? Joining the guard? It's kind of sad, really. Like, you were never young. Come to think of it, you act like you were never young. You're way stodgy beyond your years."

He kept the sting of that from registering in his face. *Stodgy?* No, not just stodgy. *Way* stodgy.

He kept his voice deliberately neutral. "I'm just saying maybe, in time, you may see it for the best that the job and engagement didn't work out exactly as you planned."

"I think you may be right. I'm not ready to be like my folks. Or you. The fun grinds to a halt the second you make a commitment." She regarded him thoughtfully. "I could show you a thing or two about having fun, Lancaster."

It occurred to him he did not know anything about her parents, beyond what was in his file on Sophie. Married for twenty-five years, settled in Mountain Bend. Were they not happy? Now was the wrong time to show interest in that, particularly since he knew she *could* indeed show him a thing or two about having fun. Again, he thanked years of discipline for not letting anything show in his face.

He noted she had dropped the Major, just as he had inadvertently dropped the Miss. Small things, but indicators he was in a tricky situation.

When she got no reaction, she gave a short laugh.

"But you're out of luck this time. I'm officially

heartbroken. I won't be coming after you," she continued, her tone deliberately light. "Reigniting the old flame. It's not in the cards. Sorry, it's probably a disappointment to you. Every man loves to have someone shamelessly besotted with him."

There was no way to respond to that without getting in trouble, particularly since she had hinted her ex might be that kind of man, so he maintained his silence. He pulled up in front of the castle and saw her reach for her door handle.

"If you'll just wait a moment, I'll come around—"

He got out of the car, but Sophie was not waiting for him to open her door for her. She flipped her hair one more time and slid quickly out of the car, as if it were a race. She opened the back door, grabbed her own bag and threw it over her shoulder.

"Miss Kettle," he said.

She waved a hand over her shoulder at him. "Don't trouble yourself. I've been here before. I know my way."

The stilettos were making it harder to make that getaway than she had probably thought it would be, and he could have easily caught up with her. She even glanced over her shoulder, daring him to come after her.

He folded his arms over his chest, and narrowed his eyes, but resisted the temptation to follow her, and escort her to the prince and princess's quarters within the castle.

Despite the fact she he had been here before, a guest traipsing through the palace unaccompanied and unannounced was not the norm. He was not at all happy she was thwarting protocol, but he had a feeling he'd better get used to it, because she was not really under his authority and he needed to get over any illusion that she was!

"Pick your battles wisely," Lancaster reminded himself firmly. He watched until she was safely inside the palace doors, and then got back in the car and drove away.

CHAPTER THREE

A WEEK LATER Sophie picked her way along the darkening cobblestone path that led away from the castle, and then zigzagged its way down the steep cliff side from the palace grounds to the village below. She paused for a moment, aware she was a bit nervous. Maybe she shouldn't have been quite so eager to slip her guard.

She ordered herself to breathe, and as she watched, lights began to come on in the buildings—many of them dating back to medieval times. It was like watching a Christmas card come to life.

She felt in her handbag for her flashlight—they called them torches here—because it would be full dark by the time she wound her way back up. She headed eagerly toward the promised warmth of those lights.

She contemplated what she was experiencing on Havenhurst—something she hadn't been expecting. She felt lonely. Adrift, almost.

Sophie, deep in her thoughts, but already a little nervous, shrieked as something moved in the shrubbery beside her.

"Miss Kettle," Lancaster said, pushing himself out of the shadows.

"Oh! You scared me!" And that was the only reason her heart was doing double time, she told herself firmly. She hadn't seen Lancaster for the entire week. Somehow, she had thought he would be more a part of daily life, or at least that she would catch glimpses of him, cross paths with him when he came to visit his godson. She was guiltily aware she even selected her outfit each day with that in mind. Even though she was definitely no longer in the market, every woman wanted to be seen as attractive by a man like him.

The truth was even though distance between them was the safest thing, she craved the company of someone she knew. Anyone! And she was glad she had on her snug designer jeans, tucked into high leather boots that might not have been the best for walking, but did show off the length of her legs to great advantage. She was wearing a gorgeous red cape against the autumn damp that was worst in the evenings, and she had a large designer bag that matched her boots.

He did not look the least contrite that he had startled her. And he did not seem to take any notice of her outfit, whatsoever. In fact, his handsome features had a distinctly sour look on them, which should have made him less attractive, but didn't. At all.

"So, Little Red Riding Hood, what if it hadn't been me lying in wait for you?" he asked, raising the dark slash of an eyebrow at her. "What if it had been the big, bad wolf?"

"Don't be silly." Little Red Riding Hood wasn't *exactly* the image she'd been trying for. His voice was so sexy it made the hair on her arms stand up.

"I'm *never* silly."

"Shocking you'd make a reference to something as lighthearted as a fairy tale, then."

"Most fairy tales are very dark if you look below the surface."

"That's something I wouldn't have considered you any kind of expert on, fairy tales."

"The Tyrant Prince has his favorites."

The thought of Lancaster reading Ryan stories filled her with *more* longing for things she didn't have. Things she had sworn off of, Sophie reminded herself firmly.

"Were *you* lying in wait for me?" she asked.

"Yes."

She looked into his face. Even in the poor light, she could see right below the slightly sour, impassive expression, a spark of anger glittered in those green eyes.

"Where's Guardsman Henderson?" he asked silkily.

Sophie shrugged. "I think he's still standing outside the powder room door on the nursery floor. Ryan's in bed for the night, and it's become my habit to go to town and have tea at that little shop Maddie started."

She loved that cozy bakery, and the cheery girls who worked there, how they were coming to know her and greeted her as if they were glad to see her.

"I'm well aware of your habits," he said tersely.

He was?

"Well, if it was anyone but you saying that, I could interpret it as downright creepy."

She was teasing him, but he did not seem receptive. She tried a different tack. She smiled at him. "Do you still love scones, Lancaster?

Come have one with me. Do you approve of my pronunciation? Scone, as in gone, not scone as in cone?"

But he wasn't being dragged down memory lane, he wasn't being put off and he didn't smile back. From the expression on his face, Sophie was guessing he was not going to be joining her for a scone.

"It's the guardsman's job to look after you," he said, his tone tight. "What do you think happens to a soldier when he doesn't do his job?"

"He's not in trouble, is he?" she asked, and felt genuinely contrite when she saw the expression on Lancaster's face. "It's not his fault. I don't like being followed around. It's unnerving and it makes people look at me sideways and afraid to approach me."

"Life isn't always about what you like. Everyone on this entire island and beyond knows you are close to the princess. That makes her vulnerable, through you."

"Oh," Sophie said. "I hadn't thought of that." She registered, slightly miffed, his concern was for Maddie.

"You think you were assigned a guardsman

because it amused me? Because I wanted to keep tabs on you?"

"Look, obviously, you're angry."

"I'm not angry."

"Oh, you are so! I'm going to have tea, so I'll wait here if you want to send Ricky to walk me to the village. Though, really, so tedious for him. He won't eat with me."

"Ricky?" he breathed. "I should bloody well hope he's not eating with you! I just came across him wandering about, looking for you, and he admitted you gave him the slip last night, too."

"I found these hot springs, not too far a walk from the castle. I'm afraid I didn't want him sneaking a peek at me while I had my lovely evening soak."

"No one under my command would ever sneak a peek at you."

"They're just men," she said.

"They are *not* just men. They are guardsmen."

"Whatever. I'm not inviting any of them to the hot springs with me. And I'm not giving it up. It reminds me of Mountain Bend." She hesitated. Really? If you had to pick someone to confide in, Lancaster would be an awful choice. But she had no choice.

"I'm homesick," she admitted softly.

"You've been here a week! And you insinuated home wasn't *fun*."

His response was not in the least sympathetic, but she felt she could not shut off the tap now that she'd opened it.

"My career and my travels gave me all the fun I needed," she said, "and going home grounded me." In fact, when she thought of the solidness of her mom and dad and the loyalty of her friends and that life being so far away she felt a sharp pang of longing…and loneliness. Even though she hadn't lived in Mountain Bend for some time, and had made a small apartment in Portland home base, it was still always only an hour away. And the quiet of it appealed to her more now than she wanted to let on.

It seemed too pathetic to admit to him that she was lonely, so she said she was bored, instead.

"Prince Ryan, while he has his adorable moments, is mostly, as you said, a royal tyrant in a two-year-old body. And he has a nanny, who seems to be worried that I'm here to take her job, so I have to tread very carefully about how much I take on with him. Thankfully, he's worn himself out by seven, because possibly I'd kill him if he was up any later than that."

"Note to self," Lancaster said, still without any sympathy at all, "threat to Prince Ryan increases after seven in the evening."

"Go ahead and make a joke out of it, but I need adult interaction."

"Your best friend is here."

"Maddie's not herself. She's under doctor's orders to remain in bed. I mean I love her dearly, but there's only so much we can chat about. Besides, I'm a sympathetic vomiter."

"A what?"

"If somebody else gets sick, I get sick, too."

"That's not a real thing," he said with authority.

"It is. Google it. And I'm afraid it's made our visits quite unpleasant."

"I'm trying not to imagine it."

"Why? If you don't think it's a real thing, imagine away. See what happens."

He glowered at her.

"It's quite a relief, actually, when Prince Edward arrives. He's not a sympathetic vomiter, by the way. He seems to find Maddie quite adorable even hunched over the loo, gagging. Anybody who thinks royal life is all glitz and glamour could have an evening with the pair of them. Sitting on the bathroom floor, eating soda crackers and giggling.

"Still, even with that, they're like the poster children for romance. They've been married forever. You'd think they'd be beyond the starry-eyed stage."

She stopped herself—barely—from saying how the couple's love for each other made her feel lonelier than ever, and a sharp sense of longing that didn't feel as if it could ever be filled.

The thunderous look was softening a bit on Lancaster's face, so she took that as encouragement and went on.

"I like to go to town for my supper—you call it tea, I know, but that's very confusing. Besides, Edward takes his meals with Maddie, feeding her off his spoon and wiping her brow, and it's all quite romantic and very intimate. Well, until she loses it again." Sophie sighed. "I can tell they cherish their time, even with the vomitus interruptus. There's nothing worse than being the third wheel at a party for two."

"You'll make some friends," Lancaster said, but she could hear the uncertainty in his voice.

Whether that uncertainty was caused because he didn't think she would make friends, or because he was out of his element trying to be sensitive, she wasn't quite sure.

"Friends," Sophie said with a snort. "I've been invited to eat with the family, if you can call it that. The dining table is a veritable football field. His mother and father are completely stuffy, and it's excruciating trying to think of things to say and remember all the rules I'm supposed to remember to dine with the king and queen. It's quite remarkable that Edward is as lovely as he is, don't you think?"

Apparently Lancaster's job description did not allow him to comment on the loveliness of his employer, because he said nothing. Which encouraged her to keep talking!

"Don't even get me started on blarneycockles! I know they're your national food or treasure or something, but do they have to be on every table? Honestly, I think that's why Maddie has taken to her bed. Perpetually nauseated by blarneycockles."

She paused for breath. "I thought I should probably go back to the US but Edward begged me not to. He said that I'm helping immensely.

That both Maddie and Ryan seem so much better since I got here."

"I believe that's true," Lancaster said, nodding
emphatically.

She cast him a faintly suspicious look. Why
did he sound eager to have her stay? He couldn't
possibly know if it was true or not, since he
hadn't even been around for the past week.

"I've committed to staying until the baby
comes, and maybe a little beyond that, but honestly, Lancaster, this is a lovely place, quite
quaint and charming, but extraordinarily dull.
It's what I left behind in Mountain Bend, only
worse because aside from Maddie, I don't have
any friends or family here. And because I'm
friends with her, the princess, none of the other
staff wants to get chatty with me, as if I'm
upper crust—there's a laugh—and they aren't.
I mean, even though Ricky was super polite
and answered all my questions—his girlfriend's
name is Becky and he has a dog named Buck—
I couldn't exactly have a conversation with him,
because he wouldn't ask anything about me. I
have to do something or I'm going to become a
raving lunatic."

He was silent.

"Quit looking at me like that, as if you think I already am a raving lunatic." It occurred to her she *had* been raving, a week's worth of pent-up frustrations boiling over on her.

"I'll walk you down to the village and have tea with you," Lancaster said.

She looked at him. She wanted to weep she was so grateful for his company and understanding. Was it possible she and Lancaster could be friends?

I doubt it, a voice inside her whispered.

She glanced at him again. As always, his face was unreadable.

"Are you escorting me? Your duty? Ricky's replacement?"

"Please stop calling him Ricky," Lancaster said with a groan. He did not answer the question.

"It's a mark of my desperation that I'll say yes to your suggestion, even though it's prompted by either a sense of duty or pity," she told him.

He looked at her long and hard. "You make me feel many things, Sophie, pity not being one of them."

Which left duty. Still…

"What kind of things?" she whispered.

"Oh, no you don't, lass. It's bad enough I've admitted to having a feeling."

She laughed at that, and it felt good to laugh with someone—anyone—though somehow laughing with Lancaster was special. Well, not exactly *with* him. She was laughing. He had what might have been a reluctant smile tickling across the full, sensuous swell of his lips.

"Those boots don't seem like the most practical," he said, finally noticing her lovely outfit, but not with approval. "And that bag must be heavy. What on earth do you put in a bag that size?"

"I have a collapsible donkey in here," she told him. "For the trip back up. It's not nearly as easy as the one going down."

He did smile at that.

A group of schoolgirls in sports uniforms were coming up the pathway toward them. Lancaster pulled back to let them by, asking them something in Gaelic.

The giggles intensified. One girl blushed. Another, beautiful with a head of flaming-red curls, stopped and said something to him. She had her hand on her hip and rocked forward slightly on one leg as she said it. Her voice was a purr and her air was definitely flirtatious.

It reminded Sophie, uncomfortably, of exactly the kind of attention her fiancé had attracted from fans at rock concerts.

But Lancaster had a different attitude. He looked at the girl sternly, then leaned very close to her, and said something for her ears only. She rocked back from him, and went very pale before hurrying off to catch up to her friends.

"What was that about?" Sophie asked.

"They're going to the pitch on the castle grounds. I told them to score one for me. That's all."

"It's not all! That's part of why I feel so lonely here. English is the official language, but the accents are so thick, or people mix Gaelic and English to the point I can't understand half of what anyone is saying."

"The girl who stopped said something quite naughty about scoring," he admitted reluctantly.

"I figured as much. And what did you say that dispatched her as if she'd been confronted with a banshee?"

"I said I knew her father."

Sophie studied his face. "Do you?"

"Good grief, no. I had no idea who she was, let alone who her father is."

"What a perfect response." Sophie laughed, partly in relief because Lancaster was so unlike her fiancé, Troy.

But then she stopped laughing. That girl, really, had been just like she had been when she first met Lancaster. Young. Intrigued. Testing a newfound feminine power. And yet, testing it on a man she knew, intuitively, was completely safe. Honorable.

Biology, she reminded herself, the power of which was not to be underestimated.

"It must be very tough on you fighting off the attentions of females, young and old," she said drily. Troy would have seen that as a compliment.

"A full-time occupation," he agreed, just as drily.

Sophie felt a reluctant trust in him. And then they shared a tentative smile. It made her aware what a rare thing Lancaster's smile was.

If she wasn't aware he was already fully occupied fighting off female attention, she might be tempted to try to make that smile happen more often.

Instead, she turned quickly to the path. He fell into step beside her, and Sophie was aware that though there was no reason to be frightened on Havenhurst—the very thought seemed ludicrous—there was something immensely solid about having Lancaster at her side. There was something about the way he moved—with an innate sense of his own power—that made her feel protected. It was a lovely feeling, even though she did not need protection!

The streetlights, charmingly old, were coming on as they entered the village. Sophie turned to go the way she always went, down a street of the most delightful thatched roof cottages, but Lancaster nodded to a different street.

"I usually go this way," he said. She could not help but notice that everyone they passed seemed to know who he was. He was admired, but it seemed people trusted him, completely, not to ever take any kind of advantage of that admiration, unlike someone else she could think of! Lancaster had earned a deep-seated respect from his fellow countrymen and women.

The way he had chosen didn't seem like the most direct route, but all the streets of Havenhurst were equally enchanting, and she readily gave herself over to exploring a new route.

"It's so old," she said.

"It is, indeed. Some of these buildings date back to the thirteenth century."

"The oldest building in Mountain Bend was from the eighteen hundreds. Look, the shops are still open."

"Traditionally, they stay open later on Friday."

It marked how her days had begun to melt together that she hadn't even realized it was Friday.

"What's this building?" she asked, pausing to look at a sign above a doorway that said Top Secret. While most of the buildings on the street were quaint—brick or stone, with steep-pitched roofs, dormer windows and soaring chimneys—this one was squat, square and formidable.

"It's kind of creepy-looking. The Havenhurst spy agency?"

He actually threw back his head and laughed. "It used to be a jail, but it's enjoying a rather heady second life. One of Havenhurst's proudest success stories."

Sophie looked up at his face, illuminated by both the streetlights and his laughter. His laughter was rich and real. She tried to think if she had heard him laugh before. She didn't think you could possibly forget if you had. He carried himself with a certain grimness, a man not to be messed with, who rarely let his guard down.

She felt just like that schoolgirl who had just tried out her feminine wiles on him. Just like the girl she had once been, she wanted to be the one whom he let down his guard for.

"What kind of success story?" she forced herself to ask.

The laughter died. He suddenly looked uncomfortable. "Let's go for that scone," he said.

She frowned at him. "There's an open sign. I'll go see."

"Wait."

Sophie ignored him, and pushed open the heavy, black iron-clad door. It had huge nail heads in it, as if she was entering a medieval torture chamber. And so nothing about the imposing exterior prepared her for what was inside. The space was beautifully lit, lights shining on gorgeous creations in silk and lace.

Top Secret. Lingerie.

She turned back to see Lancaster scowling at her from the street. It was hilarious that such a self-composed man was embarrassed about a little lingerie.

Hilarious and endearing.

Even though she was almost pathetically lonely, the last thing she wanted was to be endeared by Lancaster. She shut the door behind herself, leaving him on the street.

CHAPTER FOUR

LANCASTER WATCHED THE heavy door swing shut behind Sophie.

Could nothing with her go according to design? His protection plan for her had involved keeping a professional distance, doing absolutely nothing that could build on that undeniable electricity between them.

One week in, and Sophie had managed to totally thwart his plan, not just by giving her detail the slip, but by taking dark, isolated paths by herself and cavorting, alone and unclothed, in a hot spring.

Even though she was afraid.

That shriek, when he had startled her, and the look in her eyes, had given her away. She carried fear inside her. Was it defiance of that fear that made her take chances?

He felt a shiver go up and down his spine at the thought of someone with ill intent coming across her in either of those vulnerable states.

The fact that he sensed some fear in her made his need to protect her intensify.

And so a week in, he had to admit his original plan seemed to be sadly, and totally, in tatters.

Now, a simple walk to town for a scone had become this.

He realized, though, as much as he wanted to, he could not blame Sophie for this latest unexpected turn in events. He had chosen the route. Because he could not walk down Honeysuckle Lane, with its row of thatch-roofed cottages.

Sophie could not know that one—the one that had been razed by fire—was missing. In its place, he understood, was a tiny, but beautiful garden spot, tended lovingly by an entire community that still grieved his loss with him.

Even though nearly half a dozen years had passed, he could still see it in the faces of the people who looked at him, how they shared his pain and his sorrow.

Still, avoiding Honeysuckle Lane tonight had been one of those rare decisions that he made based solely on emotion.

And look where that had gotten him! It was a warning about the reliability of emotion. He was losing control of his charge as easily as Henderson had. Make that Ricky. With his girlfriend, Becky, and his dog, Buck.

Lancaster had not—until the moment of Sophie's reveal—known Henderson's first name. Certainly not that he had a girlfriend or a dog.

But that was the thing to remember about Sophie. She could weave a spell around a man in minutes, getting him to reveal all his secrets.

He remembered, with a sudden ache, a long, long time ago, when he and Edward had arrived in Mountain Bend, incognito. He had hurt her, and he had gone to Sophie deep in the night to tell her why. To tell her there was a stone where his heart used to be. He had told her that for *her*, so that she could understand his rejection of her was nothing personal.

And yet, after he had confided his deepest loss to her, there had been a feeling of some weight in *him* lifted.

There it was again. That word. *Feeling*. It had no place in his life, and it was probably preventing him from doing his job properly right now. Because he was standing out here on the street, like a gauche teenage boy trying to deal with his *feelings*, and she was probably in there trying to find the back door, giggling about giving him the slip just as easily as she had Henderson.

Feeling as though he was striding toward battle, Lancaster took a deep breath, crossed the walkway and shoved open the door.

The light was soft and the atmosphere in the store was frighteningly feminine. *Sensual* might not have been too strong a word. The brick walls were painted a pale pink. Tufted chairs were dotted about. There were lit glass columns displaying all manner of skimpy, lacy things.

Lancaster almost thought an alarm bell might start ringing, a robot voice shouting warning the enclave had been breached, *Man, man, man.*

He was almost sorry that Sophie was not trying to make her escape at all. She was standing, with a very elegant-looking woman, both of them focused on something the woman was holding.

They looked up when he came in, revealing what the woman had in her hands. It appeared to be a brassiere.

Which really shouldn't have surprised him. Top Secret, particularly after its endorsement from Princess Madeline, was making a name for itself around the world, exporting these highly personal feminine items.

"Oh, Lancaster," Sophie said, "you're just in time."

In time? For what? He contemplated what he was feeling. *Panic.* Flight or fight. He realized his hand was still on the door handle.

That thing Prince Edward had said he'd never seen him feel? Fear? Lancaster was feeling it now. It took every ounce of his soldier's nature to keep himself from bolting back out the door.

"I can't understand a word she's saying. I need a translator." Unless he was mistaken, there was an impish little smile tickling around the edges of Sophie's full lips.

Lips he had tasted.

Now there was a dangerous thought to be having in a lingerie shop! He could not let Sophie know she was having this effect on him. She would use it mercilessly.

The woman turned her attention to him, and recognized him. For just a moment, he saw that deep sympathy in her eyes. And then her gaze flitted to Sophie and back to him. Filled with hope.

Hope from a stranger. It felt as if it could

weaken something in him in a moment when he felt he desperately needed to be strong.

"She's my job," he told her, sternly, in their own tongue. "She can't understand you. She's asked me to translate what you're saying."

The woman nodded, clearly not convinced about the job part. "This is our most popular design," she said, holding up the item so he could see it better.

He was translating, not drawing a picture! Schooling his features to complete boredom, he relayed that information to Sophie.

Sophie actually took the item and studied it. Against his will, his eyes went back to the item in her hands. It was a confection of ivory-colored lace and soft gray mist.

"It looks so insubstantial," Sophie said doubtfully.

What did she need substantial for? he thought, making himself not look at the area in question. He had just assured her no guardsman would ever sneak a peek!

Not that he had to be sneaking peeks. He knew darn well precisely what she was built like. Her first day here she had reminded him of that exactly by falling into him. It was burned into his brain like a brand.

Do not go any further down that road, he ordered himself, *and do not blush.*

The saleslady looked askance at him.

"She says it doesn't look like it's up to the job," he said. His voice had a bit of a croak in it. *Job,* he reminded himself. *What you're here to do. Job? Earth calling Lancaster.*

"Yes," the woman said, pleased. "That's the magic of this design. The support hasn't been sacrificed for the sexiness."

He did not want to be part of a conversation about support and sexiness in women's underwear!

"She said looks are deceiving," he told Sophie. Discussing sexiness with her, in any context, was not in the job description.

Sophie turned it over in her hands, not looking convinced about the support issue, but looking enchanted all the same. Did she not own any sexy underwear? Did she have to act like she had never seen lace on a bra before?

"It's so soft," she said.

What did that mean? The one she wore was hard? He did not need to be thinking about what the one she wore was like! Thinking those kinds of thoughts would be worse than sneaking a peek!

"Ask her what her measurement is," the saleslady instructed him.

He would not!

"She should try one on."

He stared at the woman. He opened his mouth. Not a single, solitary sound came out.

"Tell her she won't believe it. It will make her feel like a woman in a way nothing ever has before."

It seemed to him that was a rather remarkable claim. He was *not* jealous of underwear. He simply was not. He wouldn't allow it.

"What?" Sophie asked him. She had a mischievous glint in her eye. She was enjoying his discomfort. Immensely. He'd had enough.

"She says she's closing. You need to come back another time." But that begged the question, with whom would she come back? Henderson? *Ricky?*

To the salesclerk he said, "Could you give her a catalog? She says it is highly personal. She'd rather order online."

The saleslady eyed him suspiciously, because Sophie's one word—*What?*—obviously did not amount to what he was saying it did. Still, his reputation helped him out, because she did not question him, but went and got a catalog and pressed it into Sophie's hands.

"Tell her there's a section in the back she must see. Our new line. Pleasure enhancers."

She had quite the twinkle in her eye. It occurred to him the clerk, while being more subtle about it, was enjoying his discomfort at least as much as Sophie.

"I would not deliberately embarrass a person by publicly discussing something so private," he said evenly, a lesson he hoped she would hear.

She was not the least contrite. What was it about him and difficult women tonight?

"Americans aren't usually so inhibited," she said, lifting a shoulder.

To his great relief they were back out in the night in seconds. The air felt cold on his cheeks, which made him realize they must have been burning.

"I heard the word *Americans*. What did she say?"

"It was an honor to have a visitor from so far away." He was unaccustomed to lying and wouldn't meet Sophie's eyes. Lying got a man into trouble, anyway. For instance, he had told her this shop was closing, and now if he didn't want her to know that was a lie, they would have to return to the pathway to the castle by way of Honeysuckle Lane.

Oh, what a tangled web we weave when first we practice to deceive.

And so his relief at getting her out of the shop was short-lived. They entered the warmth and light of the bakery and he was impossibly aware of Sophie. The counter girls greeted her as if she was a long-lost friend, and he saw her warmth and friendliness as she returned the greeting, calling one girl by name.

It was a reminder Sophie, despite the new layer of sophistication, was a wholesome, small-town girl at heart. She was not a person anyone should be having terrible renegade thoughts about what would make her feel like a woman in a way nothing had before.

"Go find a seat," he said to her. "I'll order."

"But you don't know what I want," she said.

That was true. He did not. Not in any of the multitude of ways that could be taken.

"What do you want, then?" Did his voice have

a snap to it he hadn't intended? She wasn't being unreasonable. He was.

She told him and went and found a seat. He placed the order and went to the table. He put a steaming-hot tea in front of her, and one at his place at the table. He slid into the seat across from her. Sophie ignored him completely, pouring over her new catalog.

Don't look at her, he ordered himself.

He'd been in the military for all of his adult life. For thirteen years. He was a man who knew how to obey orders. So, he looked over her shoulder, out the window and saw evening fog moving in, watched people moving down the streets, and in and out of shops.

And then he glanced at her, and the order he'd given himself was gone like that fog outside would be if sunlight hit it.

She had removed her little red riding hood thingy. He looked at the way her hair fell forward over her face, and at the slight gloss on her lips, the thickness of her lashes, the way her sweater hugged the part of herself that he was newly and uncomfortably aware of.

She looked up suddenly, turned the magazine

to him, just as scones, fresh from the oven, were set on the table in front of them.

"What do you think of this one?"

He stared at the picture she had turned toward him. It felt like the worst kind of sin that he could imagine her in *that*. He was a professional. He was a professional protector and she was the principal, in other words, his job, his mission. The one he would not sneak peeks at if she was stark naked!

"Um…" He picked up a scone, heaped a small mountain of clotted cream on it and shoved the entire thing in his mouth. He thought he was going to choke on his scone, that's what he thought of that one.

Despite the fact he had barely swallowed his first scone, was in danger of choking on it, and snorting cream out his nose, he picked up another and bit into it, as well.

She waited patiently.

"It's very nice," he managed to choke out, finally.

"Red or black?" Sophie smiled sweetly at him.

But he was revising his assumption she was wholesome. It was possible she was the devil herself.

"Are you trying to make me uncomfortable?" he asked.

"I'm just having a bit of fun."

Obviously, she was way too much for Henderson. Any ideas he had of returning the guardsman to his protection duty were evaporating.

She turned the catalog back to herself, and flipped through the pages.

"Oh," she said, her eyes suddenly widening.

Lancaster braced himself.

But she closed the catalog abruptly and put it in that ridiculous oversize bag that he suddenly felt grateful for.

"So, Lancaster," she said, her voice a touch squeaky, "tell me what you do for fun."

Nothing to do with women's underwear, he retorted in his mind, but not out loud, because he had a reputation to uphold and they were in a public place.

And possibly he could not say it without the tiniest bit of regret.

For some reason, he tried to think of ways he had fun, as if it was a test question that he was about to fail.

While she waited for an answer, she took a bite of her scone, and there was a little dot of cream clinging to her lip. After a moment, she removed it with the tip of her tongue.

It made him think of fun in a terrible new light.

"I don't have fun," he told her grimly, amazed that he hadn't given her that totally honest answer instantly.

"That's ridiculous. Everyone has fun."

He didn't say anything.

"There's a poster on the wall over there. The local pub is hosting a band coming from Ireland that plays spoons. I don't even know what that is for sure, but it has to be fun."

For a moment, he was transported to the warmth of a kitchen, shouted laughter, the *rat-tat-tat* percussion of the spoons, like a horse trotting across a wooden bridge, voices raised in song, a baby bouncing on his knee, clapping chubby hands together.

"We should go," she suggested.

We. She was going dangerous places. Far more dangerous than she knew.

"Come on," he said, scraping back his chair. "I want to show you something."

She looked at the one nibble she had left of her scone, and looked as if she was going to argue—

naturally—but then she didn't. She got up and had to put her hands way over her head to get the red thingy back on. A gentleman might have offered to help her. But he doubted there was a man on the planet who would be thinking gentlemanly thoughts after witnessing that catlike stretch.

He turned from her and she practically had to run to follow him out the door.

He turned deliberately toward the darkness in his heart that would lead him straight to Honeysuckle Lane. He would stop only briefly at that gaping hole where his life once had unfolded in normal things: a woman who waited eagerly for him, who had made him—so undeserving of the honor—the center of her life.

He wouldn't stop long enough to see a little boy in a hand-knitted jumper crawling across a swept stone floor toward him, calling out his one and only word.

"Da."

He would stop only long enough to make Sophie understand where the fun had stopped for him.

He would use it as a reminder to himself that once he had been a man who had everything, including fun. He had not treasured his life being crowded with small pleasures nearly enough when he had it. And he did not deserve to have it again.

CHAPTER FIVE

SOPHIE HAD TO scramble to keep up with Lancaster's long strides. They followed the main street out of the village square and headed down the route that she normally took.

"Of all the paths I've taken so far, this is my favorite street in the village," she told him—his back really—still scampering to keep up. "It's like something out of a storybook."

Lancaster stopped so abruptly that she very nearly crashed into him. He turned slowly and looked at her.

"Not all storybooks have happy endings, Sophie."

She was going to tell him to stop being such a sober-sided spoilsport all the time, but something in both his tone and his eyes stopped her. His gaze rested on her, somber, for a long time. Long enough that she felt a shiver go down her spine as he turned from her and faced a side yard of one of the houses.

Like the houses on either side of it, the garden was adorable. Enclosed in a low stacked-stone fence, the flower beds had been cleaned for the year, and the long-since-finished blooms cut off the shrubs, but even in the evening light, the fall color was resplendent. That beautiful autumn smell was in the air: wood smoke curling out of chimneys, crushed leaves, damp soil.

"This is where it used to be," he said, his voice low and pained.

For a moment, she didn't know what he was talking about. But when she looked at him, she felt a wave of his pain wash over her. It wasn't in his features. They were carefully schooled to show nothing at all. But there was something in his tone, his eyes, the subtle heave of his shoulders that spoke of a burden almost too great to bear, even for a man as colossally strong as Lancaster.

It occurred to her, now, that it wasn't a yard at all. It was where a little cottage had once stood, an arm's length from its neighbors.

"It's a wonder the whole street didn't go up," he said softly, his eyes moving to the thatched roofs that she had always admired as unbelievably charming.

He didn't have to say anything else. He had told her this story, once. He had been off the island on a training course. The cottages—at the time she had only imagined them, and she had not imagined anything quite so charming as this—still had the traditional open hearth and chimney in them. The ensuing investigation determined a child's toy had been left too close.

He didn't have to say anything tonight. Not about the fire. Not about his loss. She knew the message he was giving her. This was where the fun had ended for Lancaster. A man like him, who gave himself so completely, who had such a strong sense of honor and duty, might never recover from what he would see—forever—as his greatest failure.

It would make no difference to him that he wasn't there. That the incident had been totally out of his control—out of anyone's control.

That's what he was telling her.

In a way, it was a warning to her, and she knew that. But in another way, he was also trusting her with something of himself that he kept hidden, guarded from the world and the well-meaning sympathy of the neighbors.

She could see their love for Lancaster and his

family in this beautiful garden. Far back, under a tree whose branches drooped under the weight of gold and red leaves nearly the same color as Lancaster's hair, she saw a bench. It had a stone angel beside it, a winged mother who held a babe.

This wasn't a side yard to one of the cottages. Maybe she should have seen that before. These little cottages had no side yards. It was a small park. A memorial.

The sadness that gripped her was so strong, she might have wept. Except that to weep would soothe something in *her.* And there was something larger in her that asked what she could do to soothe him.

She suspected many had tried. But this place he was in was deep and dark and treacherous and she knew it was a place words could not touch. It would take amazing bravery to enter that space with him, and yet Sophie, who had never thought of herself as brave, entered unhesitatingly.

She slipped her hand into his, she connected with his agony, she accepted part of his burden as her own.

Sophie had known Lancaster for four years.

She had longed for something from him that she could not quite define.

This was the closest she had come: a moment of deep, inexplicable connection.

She thought he would feel it, too, and slip his hand out of hers immediately, but no, he accepted her hand as if he had waited for its small comfort for a long, long time. His hand was warm in hers, the strength that had been so sorely tested pulsing through it.

She was not sure anything had ever felt so right, or so pure, as standing there on a foggy street holding the hand of a man who was watching his ghosts.

Finally, he took a breath. It was long and shuddering. He let go of her hand, and turned away. They made their way silently back up the steep climb to the castle.

He did not remind her she had claimed to have a donkey in her purse. The lightness was gone from both of them. She did not speak to him at all. Sophie felt no desire to break the silence between them. The silence was a communion that felt nearly sacred.

He saw her to the door. "Please don't go to the

hot springs tonight," he said, his voice a rasp of weariness.

"I won't," she promised him. He turned to go.

She laid her arm ever so lightly on the back of his, and he turned back to her. She drank in the squareness of his chin, the silk of his fog-dampened hair, the depth of those green, green eyes. He did not pull away from her touch, but waited, returning her gaze, until reluctantly she took her hand away from his arm.

She watched him walk toward the darkness, watched with an aching heart, the power in that stride, his great sense of his confidence in being able to control the world. He had shown her his greatest failure.

It occurred to Sophie that ever since she had met him, she had seen Lancaster through the lens of herself. How he made her feel and how she wanted to feel.

But now she saw what he had possibly seen all along.

That was how a child viewed the world, seeing the world and everything in it, including people, as toys to bring them pleasure. Even her engagement had felt like an attempt to create a picture that brought her a sense of comfort, safety, belonging.

Is that why her fiancé had told her it was over? That he felt her heart wasn't in it? Because he had seen that what she called love was just an effort to make a fairy tale out of reality?

Lancaster had to have known all along, from the first time she had met him when she was eighteen and become totally and unreasonably infatuated, that her romantic view was going to meet the obstacle of reality, and be crushed.

But in this moment, it did not feel as if the reality of his sorrow was crushing her. Her heart felt both so bruised and so wide open.

And standing watching the mist swallow him whole, she had an epiphany.

What if she added a mission to her stay on Havenhurst? What if it wasn't just about helping Maddie, who didn't really seem to need her help very much, anyway? What if she was able to give a gift to Lancaster that he was sorely missing?

She thought of his laughter earlier, and how she had known what a rare thing that was. She went to bed and mulled over her plan.

* * *

The next morning she called him, using that ancient rotary dial phone in the nursery that went directly to him.

"I've decided I want to go to that Irish band thing at the pub."

Her announcement was greeted with silence.

"Spoons?" she reminded him.

"I know what you're talking about."

"I think you might want to come with me. I think me, and a few drinks, is more than poor Ricky can handle."

That should make him remember the last time he'd been with her, at the christening. He wouldn't want her inhibition unleashed on one of his guards, she was fairly certain of that. It was a mark of her commitment to this mission that she would deliberately turn his thoughts in the direction of one of her most humiliating moments.

That night came back to her. It had been absolutely magical being part of the beautiful occasion of Ryan's christening with Maddie and Edward. The connection of the prince and princess had been so strong, their love for one another shimmering in the air. Lancaster and

Sophie had been connected, also, made a couple, by the grave honor that had been bestowed on them.

Godparents. They had spoken vows over that baby that had been so like marriage vows: that they would be there for him *together* as long as Ryan needed them.

Sophie, looking at Lancaster as he held that baby so tenderly, and yet with such fierceness, had already been drunk on the feeling of *knowing* him. Knowing herself. Knowing what she wanted. And needed.

Had she remained sober, she might have kept it all to herself. But the Champagne had gone down way too easily, and she lost count of how many she had. It made her feel courageous and effervescent and unbelievably sexy.

She had seen the look in Lancaster's eyes as they had followed her. That feeling of *knowing* him had kept growing stronger as the evening progressed.

Until, finally, she had tugged him out onto a darkened balcony, bracketed his face with her hands, looked into it and felt the truth.

"You are my future," she had told him. "I've always known."

She had kissed him. And he had answered. As if he had always known, too.

But then he had put her away from him, his face the same stern face that he had shown those schoolgirls who had tried to flirt with him.

"Lass, I cannot be who you want me to be." *Canna.* And he had walked away, leaving her with a sense of drowning in her own humiliation and questioning her own intuition, the intuition that had told her, with absolute certainty, the truth about him and her and the future.

All that history leaped between them, now, over the phone wire, fierce and smoldering.

But then Sophie reminded herself how unreliable her intuition really was, because she had given it a second chance. Right until she had caught Troy with someone else she would have sworn her fiancé was devoted to her and only her.

So, this was not about rekindling anything, and Lancaster's tone, when he answered her, made her realize what a good thing that was.

"Fine," he said, his voice icy, not because of their shared history, but because he thought she had not seen what he had revealed to her last night. He thought she had not heard him at all.

He thought he had trusted her with the deepest part of himself and she was being cavalier with that trust.

In fact, she had heard him completely. And now she was going to do something she was ashamed to say she had not done very often in her life.

She was going to figure out what Lancaster needed and how to give it to him. Not to benefit herself, except that it might aid her in getting over her own sense of heartbreak and failure if she helped another person.

What did Lancaster need? The very thing he resisted the most, as if any kind of frivolity, and kind of fun, was a betrayal of the memories he held and the great loss he had sustained.

"And please don't wear your uniform," Sophie said. "It just makes me feel terribly conspicuous. As if I'm a prisoner under escort."

Silence.

"Tomorrow, then," she said. "It starts at eight. Bye."

She put the phone back in its cradle. "Buckle your seat belt, Mr. Major, the ride is about to begin."

* * *

She wasn't quite sure what a person wore to the pub in Havenhurst, so Sophie chose an outfit she would have worn to any concert, and she had been to many of them. She put on one of her favorite dresses, yellow with a parrot pattern on it. The skirt flared in a delicious swirl right at her midthigh. She coupled it with a colorful pair of cowboy boots and a denim jacket. She left her hair loose, and dabbed on just a touch of makeup.

"Really?" she told her reflection. "Girlfriend, you are practically screaming *fun*."

Lancaster, of course, was completely punctual. He looked amazing in his very lack of effort to look amazing: a casual light blue sports shirt, a brown leather bomber jacket, pressed khakis, loafers. But his expression was aloof. If he noticed how fun she looked, nothing in his eyes gave it away.

"I hoped you might wear a kilt," she said to him, trying to tease a bit of that aloofness out of him. But he was not going to be teased.

"A kilt is part of our dress uniform," he told her, his tone formal. "They are worn only for very special occasions."

He led her out to a waiting car and held open the door for her. Despite the fact he was not wearing a uniform, he seemed very much on duty. At least he held open the *front* door of the car for her.

"How was your day?" she asked, when it looked as if he intended to ignore her completely.

"Busy. Yours?"

"Peachy. You know that red fluffy bear that Ryan packs around?"

"Sammy," Lancaster said.

She shot him a look. It told her more about him than he would care to know that he knew the name of Ryan's favorite toy.

"The wonderful future sovereign of your nation flushed him. Of course, he's too large to go down. Or his head was too large. But Ryan was screaming bloody murder and the toilet overflowed and there was water running all over the nursery."

She glanced at Lancaster out of the corner of her eye. The most reluctant smile tickled his mouth.

"I'm surprised your team didn't arrive expecting terrorists, really. The nanny, Caoimhe, apparently has a phobia, so she wouldn't touch it, and she got up on a stool in a corner so as not to get her feet wet. I think she was having the vapors or something."

"Vapors? She's a trained professional," Lancaster said disapprovingly, but he was still trying not to smile.

"I'm not throwing her under the bus. Everyone has their weaknesses—remember me and vomiting?"

"Trying to forget," he said. "But vapors? Those horrible virtual cigarettes?"

Sophie could not have been more pleased! He was engaging in spite of himself.

"No, no. Not related to *vaping*. Vapors. It's an old-fashioned word for a sudden fit of fainting helplessness. Used in romance novels."

"Ah," he said, as if that explained a great deal about *her*.

"I'm not given to such things," she clarified, meaning both vapors and romance novels, though, of course, in her worst moments, that was exactly what she turned to. Romance novels, not vapors. Or vaping.

"Huh," he said, with a total lack of conviction. He seemed to remember his unspoken vow to not enjoy himself and not to add more than monosyllables to the conversation, so she gamely held it up on her own.

"That left me to extricate said Sammy from his watery trap. He came out with a tremendous pop and splatter that practically undid Caoimhe—"

"You're a bit off on the pronunciation, it's Kwee-vah."

Multiple syllables, she congratulated herself!

"Thank you. So, *Kwee-vah* was having a heart attack, and now I had a very wet and unhygienic stuffy to deal with. Ryan was leaping at me like a maddened monkey trying to get his hands on Soggy Sammy."

Sophie actually heard a muffled snort. She cast him a glance. Yes, indeed. Suppressed laughter.

"I would have liked to have passed off the cleaning and care of the bear to a qualified staff member but oh, no, Ryan, having had his friend rescued from near death, was not going to be separated. So, dragging a screaming prince, who had attached himself to one of my legs, I found the castle laundry room. Good grief, I think it used to be a dungeon. It took most of the afternoon to wash and dry the bear. Thankfully, after quite a momentous escalation of his tantrum, Ryan fell asleep on the floor. With one hand pressed firmly to the dryer that held his BFF—that's best friend forever—and one thumb in his mouth, which made it quite easy to love him again."

Lancaster had managed not to laugh out loud, but his smile was full-blown.

"And then, after Ryan went to bed, I went to see Maddie and she actually got sick seven times in a row, which I think is probably a world record, but which put me off my own dinner. So, basically I am starving, in need of adult company and ready to have a bit of fun. Thank you for asking. Will there be dancing?"

"Sorry?"

"Dancing. At the event tonight?"

"I certainly hope not," he said, his smile replaced instantly with glumness.

And then *she* laughed, and it teased another most reluctant smile out of her escort.

"There will be dancing," he said. "It's our way. But I'm afraid you will probably just want to be a spectator."

"Look at this dress," Sophie said. "Does it look like something someone who wants to spectate would wear?"

He considered this, not even trying to hide his

trepidation. It was clear, if he could think of a way out of this, he would.

But he parked the car, and walked down a cobblestone street to the pub. It had a sign out front that announced it was the Black Cauldron Free House, established in 1586.

"Oh!" Sophie said. "Another incarnation of the Black Kettle."

It was like something off a postcard: the building was a Tudor style that seemed to be leaning capriciously to one side. They stepped inside.

"It doesn't look like it's changed much in the ensuing four hundred or so years," Sophie called to Lancaster over the noise of rambunctious patrons. The floor was stone, and uneven. The ceilings were low, and the place was being held up by blackened beams that looked as though they had survived a fire. Long, rough tables were set out in rows.

She glanced at Lancaster. His eyes were narrow as he surveyed the very crowded premises. He was in warrior mode.

She could not help but notice the looks that were sent their way. He might as well have worn his uniform. Everyone knew who he was, and it made them curious about her.

She had intended to give him a carefree evening, to coax him to have some fun, but she clearly saw that this particular venue was only making him more alert, more on guard, more on duty.

"It doesn't look like there's any room," she said, disappointed.

Lancaster already had his shoulder against the door, eager to leave.

But then, just when Sophie thought her plan to coax Lancaster to have some fun had been thwarted by an uncooperative universe—who was she to decide what anyone else needed, after all—someone called his name.

CHAPTER SIX

"MAJOR! WE'LL MAKE ROOM. We have a table over there."

"Ricky!" Sophie cried, as the young guardsman appeared in front of them. It was so nice to know someone in this sea of strangers.

Lancaster cast her a look that warned her off greeting him with a hug. He looked at the door once more, with such longing that Sophie was not sure if dragging him out to this event was the right thing to have done, after all.

Ricky led them through the impossibly crowded room to a long wooden table. Men and women slid along benches until there was just room for them to sit shoulder to shoulder with their new companions. She was squished right up against Lancaster's side, and some of her confidence about whether this was the right thing to have done returned.

It felt wonderful to be sitting beside him at the crowded table. She glanced at his face to see if he shared her take on it, but as always, his expression was very difficult to read.

Introductions were shouted out—lots more tongue-twisting names—and she realized that these were men of the guard, here for a social night out with their wives and girlfriends. She could tell almost all of them were surprised to see Lancaster. Even though they were looking warily askance on each other, as if his presence might subdue the revelry, she could not help but notice that the men reacted to him with respect, and that the women were as totally aware of him as those teenage girls had been on the pathway the other day.

And again, Sophie could not help but notice that women being aware of him did not seem to stroke his ego in the least.

Thick glasses were passed down the table and set in front of them, and filled from a pitcher of dark beer.

She tasted hers tentatively. It was warm but surprisingly flavorful with rich tones of malt and caramel. Still, she vowed to be very careful tonight. Despite her using past behavior as a threat to get Lancaster here, Sophie vowed there would be no repeat performances of the christening evening.

From somewhere, a glass of water appeared in front of Lancaster, so his comrades knew he was working, and that she was his job, not his date.

Sophie did notice he had relaxed a little, though, perhaps feeling her protection was no longer his alone, now that they were surrounded by fellow members of the guard.

Though Sophie could barely understand a word spoken around her, accents thickening even more as the beer disappeared, she was still thoroughly enjoying the feeling of being with Lancaster, a part of his community.

And then, the huge hall suddenly went silent.

A lone man appeared on the stage and took a seat on a stool. He began to play a pair of long-handled wooden spoons, a primitive, steady rhythm, hand to leg, hand to leg. The hall was completely silent as he practiced this ancient art, picking up tempo, his hand moving faster and faster until it was a blur of motion, creating an amazing percussion of sound. The hall erupted into applause when he'd finished. Then, it was as if a sign had been put out: start the party.

The spoon player was joined on stage by others now, and Lancaster leaned close to her so that she could hear him, and named the instruments. He told her the violin was referred to as a fiddle, and played differently in these circumstances. There was also a *bodhran*, which he explained was a handheld drum made of goatskin and played with a wooden "tipper." There was a man with a tin whistle, one with a concertina, which was similar to an accordion, and a woman carried what he called *uilleann* pipes, which were a version of bagpipes.

Really, Sophie thought, Lancaster could read the phone book and that accent would make it sound sexy! She loved the sound of his voice in her ear, but soon her ears were filled with the leaping melodies of Celtic folk music.

A song was recognized and was met with shouts of approval. And then the entire hall was singing along, beer glasses raised, the crowd swaying from side to side along the benches, beer slopping happily onto the tables.

There was no sense asking Lancaster what the words were. She could not have made her voice heard. The noise was the most thunderous and joyous that Sophie had ever heard. There were songs the entire audience knew how to play and the wooden spoon sets were dug out of pockets, and the people played along in perfect rhythm until it sounded as if the hall was filled with stampeding horses.

The man on the other side of Sophie, older than Lancaster but just as big—she thought his name was Brody—looked askance at Lancaster and, at his nod, gave her his wooden spoons, shouting incomprehensible instructions in her ear. She tried valiantly to follow them, as Lancaster's team cheered her on. They whistled their approval at her effort when the song finished, and she surrendered the spoons, vowing, silently, to get her own set when an opportunity presented itself.

She glanced at Lancaster and saw that despite himself, he was enjoying the evening. His handsome features had relaxed, the guard that was always up in his eyes had come down a bit.

A girl joined the band on stage—a moment the crowd had obviously been waiting for. To the accompaniment of a fiddle, she did a solo jig, arms at her sides, upper body stiff, short skirt swirling, feet flying in a blur of motion.

And then, as though a signal had been given, tables were shoved back to clear the floor in the front of the stage, and lines of men and women went forward, facing each other, their upper bodies held stiffly, but their feet on fire as they jigged intricate, flying steps. Their own table emptied of a number of people.

So this was what Lancaster had meant that she might prefer to be a spectator! She hated to admit he had been right, but the people of Havenhurst had obviously been passing these complex dances from generation to generation since the beginning of time. It would be uncomfortable and awkward to be up there. She found herself content to watch, happy in her awareness that Lancaster's feet were tapping to the fast, stirring rhythms.

"Sir?"

Over the incredible noise, she heard someone addressing Lancaster. Sophie realized it was Ricky. He was looking quite flushed, perhaps from having too many beers. He had his arm draped over the shoulder of a lovely girl.

"Becky says you canna bring the lass here and not teach her our dances."

Under the music, there was a sudden silence as the men who remained at their table considered Ricky, and his challenge, cleverly made through

Becky, to their leader. Sideways glances were sent toward Lancaster.

Was it possible, Sophie wondered, holding her breath, that there were many people besides herself who longed to see Lancaster's light come back on?

Lancaster leveled Ricky a look that could have stripped paint. The young soldier suddenly looked quite a bit more sober.

But then, Lancaster lifted a shoulder and tilted his head toward Sophie.

"Are you game?" he asked her.

She glanced back up at the people dancing, at their flying feet and their ingrained sense of these dances.

She really was not game! She was going to look a total fool.

But then she remembered why she had come here, that it wasn't about her at all. It was about moving Lancaster back toward his own light. He was offering to dance with her. Did it really matter what the circumstances were?

When Lancaster held his hand out to her, and she took it, her fear of appearing a fool dissipated. It felt as though if there was ever a man in the world you could trust to look after you, it would be this one. His hand taking hers felt, just as it had the other night, when they stood at the cottage site, like the most right thing that had ever happened to her.

Still, when his hand closed around hers, and his simple strength was conveyed to her, she knew that it was this belief that he—and others—had in his strength that was at the very core of what had broken his heart. He had been trusted, and he had failed.

Even though it had not been his fault.

Maybe this was how she could be instrumental in helping him rebuild his trust in himself. Just one tiny step—even if it was a dance step—at a time.

Sophie's hand was in his *again*, Lancaster thought, bemused. After the other night, when he had felt the astonishing comfort and strength when her hand had found his in front of that terrible place where the cottage had burned, he had made a vow.

No more.

It was a weakness to accept what she offered. It was a weakness because it opened a door that was better left shut.

When she had called him, the next day, it had seemed as if that vow would be easy to keep, indeed. How could she even ask him to come to something like this? How could she have missed the point of the depth and breadth of his sorrow so completely? How could she have missed the point that it had altered him? He had fallen off the wall, and there was no putting him back together again.

And yet now his hand closed around hers, again. And by his own invitation!

He needed to remember this about Sophie: a vow could fall around her as easily as a tree before a logger's ax.

But perhaps even more astonishing than the fact her hand was in his again, was the fact that he had hated the thought of coming here tonight.

And yet now that he was here, the music and the songs and the sense of joyous community called to some part of him that he had left sleeping for a long, long time. He felt something in him, long held tense, relax, as the music swirled and he lined up next to Sophie, instead of across from her, on the dance floor.

It was too loud to really instruct her, and the

dances were fast moving, familiar to every person here, except her.

She was hesitant, uncharacteristically self-conscious.

He dropped his lips close to her ears so that she could hear him above the racket. "Just relax. Try not to think about it too much."

"Everyone's watching me. They think I'll make a fool of myself, and I will."

This seemed to be something new about her, Lancaster thought. In all the years he'd known her, there had never been any shortage of confidence. Now, even though she had that new layer of sophistication, something had knocked her down a peg or two.

The lost fiancé and job, no doubt.

"They're watching you because you're bloody gorgeous," he said, firmly, "and I don't think anyone on Havenhurst, including me, has ever seen a dress like that before. At least not with Western boots."

She laughed and tossed that shining black wave of hair over her shoulder. He thought, *That's more like it*, as he felt, in that simple gesture, how effortlessly she drew all the male attention in the room to herself.

Still, her effort to replicate the steps he showed her was hesitant at best.

"I should have encouraged you to drink more," he said, with a sigh. "Now, don't pay any attention to them. Just me."

He quickly regretted that when her eyes locked on his, and he could feel himself pulled toward her as if she was a lifeboat and he was a man drowning. Just a second! He was saving her at the moment.

From what? a voice deep inside him whispered.

"My feet?" he suggested.

"Oh!" she said, and blushed before she looked down.

Ignoring the tempo of the music and the swirl of motion around him, he took her through a very basic step sequence, again, thanking his gods that the beginning sequences did not involve any kind of contact between them, because his awareness of her made him feel raw and open.

"That's good," he said.

She beamed at him—a look a man could live for and want to spend the rest of his life coming home to—and some hiss of pure chemistry leaped in the air between them. It mixed him up about the next sequence, and Ricky's lass came over, and watched critically.

"Ach. You big oaf," she said. "Get out of the way."

He stared at her in stunned silence for a moment, and then stepped back with a slight bow and great relief.

Where had that thought come from? That Sophie was a girl a man could want to spend the rest of his life coming home to?

It turned out Becky was the natural-born dance teacher who Lancaster was not. Under her tutelage, Sophie caught on extremely quickly. No doubt that lack of that sizzling hiss of chemistry helped in the instruction process!

"That's it," Becky called, as she faced her, dancing, and got Sophie to mirror her moves. "Toe, heel, toe, heel, right kick, left kick, turn. I meant turn the other way."

Both women howled with laughter at Sophie's missteps, and then a circle of women formed around them, clapping and encouraging them. And then the whole circle was dancing, fanning out into a line that snaked through the tables and benches, and Sophie and Becky were absorbed in all that feminine color and motion as the watching men roared their approval.

After that, it felt to Lancaster as if it was just a full-time job trying to figure out where she was. Every man in the place wanted to meet her, face off with her, loop arms with her. Many of the dances involved switching off partners multiple times, and he would catch sight of that yellow dress, with its crazy parrot pattern, through walls of people, see that fabric swirling around slender legs. He could hear her shout of laughter, catch glimpses of her face, flushed with excitement, her hair flying, no longer the least embarrassed by how she was messing up the dances.

No one else cared either. She was gorgeous and her confidence had been restored. She was in her element. As Lancaster watched, she took off her coat, tossing it carelessly into the crowd. She was in her element. Sophie was the life of the party. And as far as he could tell, except for that first sip, her drink was untouched at their table.

He saw a man holding her a little too long when he should have let go, and he saw something flash in her face. More than discomfort. Fear? He quickly stepped in, sending the man on his way, and when he looked to Sophie he felt he might have misread the situation. She was as effervescent as champagne bubbles. And yet, after that he watched even more closely, and performed several more interventions.

As the evening went on, as Sophie relaxed more and more, he felt himself becoming more and more alert as more alcohol was consumed and inhibitions were careening out the door. The night was becoming more wild and raucous with each passing minute. Men who had had too much to drink and were flushed with the excitement in the room were hovering around Sophie.

Well, this was Lancaster's job. It was what he had come to do. Protect her. She had been right. It wasn't the kind of job he would have wanted to leave to Ricky.

Yet another man dropped his head to her, saying something in her ear. Lancaster felt a furious need to know what had been said, especially when Sophie beamed at the man as if he had put the bloody sun in the sky this morning.

Havenhurst boys loved to ask a pretty girl to step out. Of course, Sophie would have no idea what that meant. She might think it was just an invitation for a breath of fresh air. Or worse, she might like the idea of... Lancaster shoved bodies out of the way to intercede, but just as he arrived, the man turned toward him.

It was Brody. Who was here with his wife of over twenty years. He would no more be inviting Sophie to step out than he would be inviting her on a trip to the moon.

Why had Lancaster arrived at that erroneous conclusion so swiftly? Brody gave Lancaster a nod of acknowledgment, then left Sophie.

Lancaster felt frozen in his tracks as a realization hit him. He hadn't moved toward Sophie with such swiftness because he was protecting her.

Or at least not entirely.

He considered a horrible—and foreign—possibility.

Was he jealous?

"Have you come to dance with me?" she asked. Her very eagerness made his heart leap in a way it had no right to.

"No, I was going to suggest we leave. Are you ready to go?" he asked her, his tone clipped.

She obviously was not. "Will it go on much longer?"

"They could go all night. I have to work to-morrow."

"Oh. I guess I do, too. One wouldn't want to be tired around Ryan. Who knows what could get flushed! I have to find my jacket."

It spoke to the growing drunkenness in the hall that they found her jacket being worn like a babushka by a reveler. He surrendered his new-found headgear reluctantly, but without a fight after a single look from Lancaster.

On their way out they passed a table full of men, not members of the guard and so not under his control. They were absolutely besotted with her, and inebriated enough to not be intimidated by Lancaster. They begged her to stay.

"Lass, I haven't danced with you yet."

"I'll die if I go home before claiming a dance."

"Have you ever kissed a Havenhurst lad? I could be your first."

She thought it was funny, until one of them grabbed her, and then he saw a look of panic on her face. This time he knew he was not mistaken, even though she covered it quickly.

Lancaster took a firm grip on Sophie's elbow

and got her by that table. He was aware he felt as though he wanted to smash something. Preferably heads together!

CHAPTER SEVEN

FINALLY, LANCASTER GOT Sophie safely outside, past the obstacle of her many new admirers. He felt as if he had run a gauntlet, with the twist of having a prize to guard, which everyone wanted. He herded her toward the vehicle.

"I know everyone is speaking English," Sophie said, "but I can only understand about every second word. No, make that every tenth word."

Kiss, Lancaster thought darkly. *Did you understand kiss?*

Not that he could go there, right now. Or ever.

Despite that vow, his eyes drifted to her lips, which looked full and plump, the color of pomegranate juice. They could appear under the heading *Temptation* in an illustrated dictionary.

"That was so much fun," she said breathlessly, seemingly determined to hide the fact something had truly frightened her. She appeared to be oblivious to his darkening mood. "My feet hurt. I think I have blisters. Can you look?"

"I cannot," he said grimly. He realized his hand was still on her elbow, and he let it go as if the touch of her skin had burned him.

Jealous? Him? That was ridiculous. More than ridiculous.

But he thought of that brief moment of chemistry that had sizzled between them at the beginning of the dance, that renegade thought he'd had about her look, that a man could live for a look like that and want to spend the rest of his life coming home to it, and he felt a moment of appalling self-realization.

He deliberately did not look at her again as she walked—limped—beside him. She probably really did have blisters. Should he look? When they got back to the palace? As a soldier, he knew a blister, a small thing, had to be looked after immediately, before it became a large thing.

But then he could imagine kneeling before her, sliding that boot off, the tininess of her foot in his hand…

Terrible thoughts. Completely inappropriate. Talk about small things becoming large things! If he was not very, very careful, this thing was going to go seriously off the rails.

"Connal!"

At first he didn't even react. It was a common enough name, after all. But then Sophie startled beside him, and he felt a hand on his shoulder. He was instantly alert. His hand went to the hilt that wasn't there—his first thought of protecting Sophie. And then it fell away as he spun and recognized his cousin.

Calum clapped him on the shoulder. "I thought I saw you in there. I should know better than to come up behind you, man. How are you?"

The two men embraced.

"I haven't seen you since—"

It hung there between them. The funeral. There it was. The reason Lancaster needed to keep this thing with Sophie from going completely off the rails.

"Who's your lass?"

Yes, that was a good question. Who was this lass to him?

He avoided the question. "Sophie, this is my cousin Calum."

"You look alike," Sophie said, and offered her hand.

Calum, of course, had to be an idiot because that was a genetic quality in the Lancaster family. He bowed over her hand, took it and kissed it. Deeply. There was that little twitch again. *Please not jealousy.*

"My mum misses you something fierce," he said, when he straightened and looked at Lancaster. "Did you know Mackay had a babe? That's my brother," he said to Sophie. "Come to the christening party. Please. It's on Saturday evening at Mum's."

Calum turned to Sophie. "Has he taken you to a proper *ceilidh*?"

"I'm afraid the only place he's taken me is to—" She stopped and looked mischievously at Lancaster. For an awful moment, he thought she was going to name the underwear shop. But she didn't. She said, "Here."

Would it just be plain churlish to say *We are not dating*?

"I don't understand that word," Sophie said. "Kay-lee?"

Of course she massacred the pronunciation, and Calum looked ridiculously charmed.

"You're American?"

"Yes, I'm here visiting my friend Maddie."

Calum should have been rocked back a bit by that, Lancaster thought darkly. A friend of the princess's really was not going to be a friend of his. But oh, no.

"A *ceilidh* is a party. You haven't really experienced our culture until you've been to one. Will you bring her?" he asked Lancaster.

"We'll see," Lancaster said.

"We'll be there," Sophie declared, ignoring his glare. Completely.

After Calum had walked away, Lancaster took her by the elbow, again, and ushered her firmly to the car.

"I won't be able to go. To the christening *ceilidh*," he said steadfastly once he had started the car. "I have a previous commitment."

He did not, and he should have known by now there was a price attached to telling innocent lies to her.

"Oh, that's fine," Sophie said sweetly. "I'm sure you can detail someone else to take me."

"You'd go to *my* cousin's party on your own?"

"Calum invited me," she said simply. "He wants me to experience your culture."

Hidden in there was the little knife of suggestion, inferring he, Lancaster, would deprive her of that experience for no reason except basic mean-spiritedness.

"I'll rearrange my schedule," he was astonished to hear himself say.

"By the way, I like your name," Sophie said thoughtfully, turning the tables on him in a blink. "I'm not sure why you're so secretive about it. I thought maybe it was an embarrassing name like Percival, or one that could be perceived as a girl's name, like Marion."

"Those are both perfectly good names," he said sternly.

"But not for you."

What did *that* mean? He was not going to give her the pleasure of asking.

"I like the sound of it. Connal," she said, and then as if it hadn't whispered across his spine like a silk scarf of sensuality, she said it again. *Connal.*

"Would you stop?" he snapped, and then had the decency to be embarrassed that he had snapped at her for no real purpose.

She regarded him thoughtfully, and then said softly, "It isn't really because you don't want people to know your first name that you don't use it. It's because you don't want people to get close to you. A first name is a highly personal thing, isn't it?"

He said nothing.

"I suppose it means something? All your names seem to mean something."

Really? He didn't want her to know his first name, he didn't want her using it, he didn't want her analyzing why he didn't give it to people, he didn't want her knowing its meaning.

And he certainly didn't want to go to his cousin's *ceilidh* with her.

He felt much angrier than any of those things warranted.

He must have managed to make her a tiny bit miffed, too, because when they arrived at the palace, she opened her own door without waiting for him to do it for her, and slammed it a little harder than might have been necessary. She didn't say good-night.

"Hey," he got out of the car and called to her. "Don't go to the hot springs tonight."

She didn't even turn back.

"Do you hear me?"

No response. A guardsman on the door opened it for her, but Lancaster didn't start the car again until he'd seen the door swing close after the little yellow dress had swished through it.

Why did he feel so angry?

It was obvious. Because Sophie Kettle was shaking his sense of being in control, even over himself.

And he did not like it. He did not like it one little bit.

He got out of the car and strode up to the door. "Call me if she leaves here," he told the guardsman tersely.

If the guardsman was in any way surprised by the reiteration of instructions he already had, unlike Lancaster tonight, he was enough of a professional not to show it.

"Yes, sir," he said.

"Hot springs, indeed," Sophie muttered to herself. She was exhausted and her feet hurt.

She made her way through the now familiar passages of the palace to her own suite. There she yanked off the boots, and then peeled off her socks, and winced at what she saw.

Blisters.

"Well," Sophie told herself, "that went well. Not!"

And she was not referring to her blisters, either. She put a few inches of hot water in the tub, and sat on the edge of it, soaking her feet and contemplating the evening.

She had actually been congratulating herself on achieving a modicum of success. Even one of Lancaster's guardsmen, Brody, had thanked her for getting Lancaster out.

"It's good to see the lad among us again," he had said.

But then "the lad"—good grief, who looked at a mountain of a man like Lancaster and saw a lad—had appeared, and everything in his face and the way he had been holding himself had said the party was over.

He'd been angry about something even before they'd met his cousin, even before his cousin had revealed his name, even before she had announced she would go to the *ceilidh* without him.

Sophie reminded herself, with a sigh, the goal had been to help Lancaster have fun.

Thinking of the look of thunder on his face as he drove her silently home, she thought her grade was probably an F. She should probably give up on her plan to save Lancaster from a dour life. It was a mission that seemed more hopeless than when she had set out tonight.

Of course, partway through the mission, she'd

totally forgotten it was supposed to be about Lancaster, and just given herself over to the pure merriment of the evening. Except for that man grabbing her at the end, and that moment of overwhelming panic until she had remembered Lancaster was there, the outing had been perfect. The music, and the dancing, the joyous spirit of celebration in the room, had been totally contagious. It was the first time since her breakup that she had glimpsed the possibility she might be happy again.

Forever single, but happy, she told herself firmly.

So, she had found hope for herself, but failed in her mission to Lancaster.

"I think you are selfish and self-centered at heart," Sophie assessed herself glumly. She took her feet out of the tub, toweled them off and then went and grabbed her computer.

Internet tonight! It was spotty on Havenhurst at best.

Surrendering the utter weakness of it, she typed in *meaning of the name Connal*. It was, as she had thought it would be, a pure Celtic name.

And it meant mighty, ferocious, respected and respectful.

Who looked into the face of a tiny newborn baby and knew these things of him? Knew he would grow into that name, and be all those things, even as he left the name behind him?

Sophie put down her computer, put on her pajamas and climbed into bed.

Just before she slept, it occurred to her that maybe the evening had not been such a total failure after all.

Lancaster had enjoyed parts of the evening, maybe even most of it. She had seen his toes tapping to the music, seen him watch the dancing with enjoyment.

Had it been when Brody had spoken to her that something had shifted in Lancaster? Had he overheard the words, then?

Had he been angry *with himself* for letting his guard down, for giving himself over to the evening, for coming back among the people who held him in such respect, but also pitied him his loss?

Even anger was movement, Sophie realized. He was a man who was contained. He prided himself on control. He had disciplined himself to feel nothing.

So even anger was a step in the right direction, wasn't it?

So, not an F.

"C minus," she upgraded herself sleepily. It wasn't a complete fail, after all. Plus, he'd agreed to accompany her to the *ceilidh*, even if he had done so grudgingly. She realized it was all the encouragement she needed. She wasn't ready to give up on Lancaster's happiness just yet.

CHAPTER EIGHT

As SHE CHOSE an outfit for the *ceilidh*, Sophie reminded herself it was about Lancaster's enjoyment, not her own. So, she'd tone it down. Casual. Not drawing attention to herself.

Still, one had to show respect for the hosts. She could hardly show up in yoga pants and a T-shirt.

She put on an oversize soft white cashmere sweater with a cowl neckline, a pencil-line skirt and low heels that were painful in two respects. Her modest height remained modest. And her feet hurt. Sneakers, unfortunately, were out of the question.

The outfit, she decided, might have been too subdued. When she met Lancaster at the car, he seemed totally focused on her feet!

"Are you suffering from blisters, lass?"

When he called her *lass* in that sexy, deep voice, it tickled along the back of her neck as if he had touched her, somehow making it okay that he had not even said hello, and that he was focusing on her feet!

"Yes. The boots the other night were a mistake."

He held open the car door for her, then slid into his side.

"What are you doing about them?"

He was thinking of her feet and she was so aware of him: the forest scent, the squareness of his wrist as he touched the steering wheel, the clean lines of his profile. She looked away from him before he caught her peeking.

She tried to focus on the question. What was she doing about what? Her wayward thoughts? No! The blisters.

"I'm soaking my feet in hot water every chance I get."

"The hot springs would be good. The minerals are very healing."

Something in his tone made her glance back at him. Maybe he wasn't quite as focused on her feet as she had thought, because unless she was mistaken, the inscrutable Major Lancaster was blushing ever so slightly.

She decided a trip to the hot springs was in her

very near future, but she mustn't be distracted by that.

Today was her chance to redeem herself. To help Lancaster back to the land of the living.

Though, really? She was not sure what would make either of them feel more alive than being in the hot springs together!

She recognized she was getting off track in a very dangerous way.

His aunt's home was a modest stone house on the edge of Havenhurst, already surrounded by cars and bicycles, the sounds of merriment spilling out every time the door opened.

Lancaster gave her a warning look when she reached for her own door handle, and because today was about making him happy, she sat there feeling like an idiot until he came around and opened her door.

Then he went to the trunk and opened it, retrieved what was inside.

Her eyes went very wide.

"You've stolen Sammy."

"It's my standard gift for a christening," he said.

She registered that Lancaster had given the young prince his favorite toy. Was it because it had been given to him by his godfather that he loved it so?

Sophie realized she had not even thought to bring a gift. So much for giving up her self-absorbed ways!

"It can be from both of us," he said, reading her sudden embarrassment with discomforting accuracy.

She cocked her head at him. "But then people will think we're a couple."

He scowled at that, and tried to give her the bear, anyway, but she shook her head. He had an ulterior motive, she was certain. She was not going to spare him—warrior-like, self-contained, utterly masculine—the discomfort of walking into the gathering of his friends and family with an adorable teddy bear riding in his big, strong arms.

She was pretty sure, from the awkward way a plaid bow had been attached to the bear's neck, no one was going to think it was from her regardless of what he said.

They entered the house, and Lancaster was met with shouts of greeting from the men, and squeals of delight from the women.

Sophie quickly realized this was his *other* life, where everyone called him by his name.

She soon lost track of who everyone was, and how they were related to him. He was absorbed into the crowd and Sophie did not want to intrude on what seemed to be a reunion of sorts. Everyone wanted to hug him, and to talk to him, as if he was the focus of this gathering, not the baby whom she had yet to lay eyes on.

Somewhere along the line, Lancaster managed to lose the bear, but not before the sight of him with it had melted every female heart in the house, whether they were six or sixty.

Children, in particular, were scrabbling for his attention, and it seemed, as she watched, he was always bending, picking one up, throwing him or her in the air and then planting a quick kiss on a cheek before putting them back down and sending them on their way.

"We meet again."

She turned to see Lancaster's cousin had come up behind her.

"Calum," she said. "Nice to see you again."

"Have you met everyone?"

"I haven't. I'm kind of hiding because I've a way of massacring names."

He smiled at her. "Thank you for making him come."

"What makes you think that I made Lancaster come?"

He laughed. "You canna call him Lancaster here. At least forty people will answer you. I know you made him come because we have not seen him for a long while."

"I wonder why?" she said, softly. "You'd think all this love would help."

"You know about his tragedy, then. I think it's the wee ones who do him in."

They both turned to watch just as the babe whom this event honored was put in Connal's arms.

Sophie noticed a deep comfort in how Lancaster held the baby. Only a man who had had a child of his own held a baby like that, with no tension, sure of himself, completely confident in his ability to adapt his strength to this delicate task.

Lancaster and the baby regarded each other solemnly for long enough for Sophie's heart to feel as if it would break in two.

"Ah," Calum said, watching her, "it's like that, then."

"Like what?" she said, brushing defiantly at the tear that raced down her cheek.

"You're joining a long lineup, lass. The other reason I think he doesn't come to the gatherings."

"I—I—don't know what you mean," she stammered.

"But you will," Calum said. "Come on. I will introduce you to me mum. She'll be delighted to have such an exotic creature in her home."

"I'm not exotic!"

"You are to us. A friend of the princess, and an American to boot! And don't worry about pronouncing names. Everyone will just be charmed by your accent."

"Promise you won't make me eat a blarney-cockle," she said, relieved they had moved away from the topic of the only Lancaster in the room who stood out to her.

Calum took her completely under his wing, and he was right about his mother's—and everyone else's—reaction to her. It was a little embarrassing, but Sophie was treated like a celebrity.

And, unfortunately, Calum was right about her understanding why Lancaster avoided his family gatherings. Just as at the pub the other night, the celebration grew wilder. The furniture was pulled back. There was singing, and spoon playing and dancing.

And it was soon apparent that to every single woman here, the star of that show was not the baby.

It was Connal Lancaster.

Calum caught her watching as yet another beautiful young woman threw her arms around Lancaster, took both his hands, tried to persuade him onto the dance floor.

"He's a romantic figure," Calum said. "A widower. A soldier. Not hard to look at. He walks with kings and yet remains of the earth. A lot of the girls here have their sights set on being the next missus."

Sophie noticed that Lancaster didn't seem to *not* be enjoying the attention.

In fact, more than once, she heard his shout of laughter, saw him tilting his head toward some gorgeous young woman, a little smile tickling across his lips.

This is what she had wanted, she told herself. She had wanted to see Lancaster relax, enjoy himself, have fun.

But it was a complete lie. It was *not* what she

wanted. It stung. It brought back terrible memories of Troy, lapping up the attention his position with the band had given him.

Except that Lancaster's interactions were different from how Troy's had been. Looking back, she should have seen that Troy's flirtatiousness with other women had a certain openness to possibilities that she could clearly see Lancaster's did not. There were no casual touches. He paid equal attention to women of every age, to men, to children. He did not linger in conversation, even with the loveliest of those who vied for his attention.

And yet… Was she jealous?

"You needn't worry about him going home with any of them."

Sophie's mouth dropped open at how she carried Troy's betrayals with her to be so easily spotted by a nearly complete stranger! Still, Calum was right. He had spotted her worry, the residue of a relationship where trust had been broken. Sophie found herself glad, for the first time, that she was Lancaster's job. Despite Calum's saying she didn't have to worry about it, she was glad Lancaster couldn't dump her and leave with someone else.

"He's become quite the legend at saying no. I think it makes some of them see him as even more of a challenge."

Something snaked along her spine. No denying it any longer. Jealous.

And angry with herself for being jealous. Because, really? You could just lump her in with all the rest of *some of them*.

"I think he's pretty much only got one love left."

"And who is that?" Sophie asked. Was her voice strangled?

"Not who. What. He loves to fish. I think it's saved him, really. As much as anything else."

All these years she'd known him, and she had not even managed to ferret that one piece of personal information out of him? That he loved to fish?

"And here he is," Calum said, "the man of the hour."

She thought he meant Lancaster. Unfairly, if it was Lancaster, she felt as if she wanted to slap him. Not for reminding her how fickle men could be, because she knew, at some deep level, he would never be like that. No, she felt angry at him for just for being too…everything. Sexy. Good-looking. Strong. Contained.

Thankfully, it was not Lancaster.

A fat baby had been plopped into Calum's arms. Like Lancaster, he seemed very comfortable with the baby. "This is my nephew Rowan."

Before Sophie could properly prepare herself, the baby was placed in her arms. Unlike the two men, she didn't feel comfortable at all. She had seen Ryan when he was a baby, but not enough to give her that natural way of dandling the baby as if he was just an extension of herself.

Rowan was a surprisingly solid little fellow, with one shock of bright red hair. He seemed to be in no danger of breaking, and he was apparently quite used to being handled by strangers. He looked up at her, and gurgled. Then cooed. His eyes were that startling shade of green that seemed to repeat in the Lancaster family over and over again.

He wagged his pudgy arms at her, then tested each of his legs. And then he smiled.

The longing she felt was so sudden, it felt as if she couldn't breathe. She passed the baby quickly back to his beaming uncle.

"I have to go outside for a minute," she said.

Calum looked at her with concern. "Are you unwell?"

"It happens. Sharing a room with blarneycockles." She tried to make light of it, but she managed to give Calum, who was still holding the baby, the slip. She found her way out the door and took deep, gulping breaths of the clean air.

But it didn't help. The weight of the baby felt as if it had wormed its way into her heart, and made her feel bereft in a way she had not even known she was capable of.

For a young woman from a small town, she had achieved so much. She'd had a great career and would again. She'd traveled the world. She was in the inner circle of a royal family. Even right now, she was living in a palace!

But holding the baby had made her aware that none of those things had ever fulfilled her. Inside her, in a place that had been secret, she still harbored the most simple of dreams. A man who loved her unreasonably and a tiny house filled with the laughter of children.

Strangely, when she'd been engaged, they had been a sophisticated couple. Well-heeled and well traveled, there had been no pleasure money couldn't buy. She'd eaten at the best restaurants, been to the best shows, vacationed in the most exclusive places.

Of course they had talked about children. What engaged couple did not talk about children? But, it had been a far-off *someday* where the imaginary children slipped seamlessly into their busy, successful lifestyle.

Seeing Lancaster surrounded by all those adoring women had put her own teen crush on him in perspective but also sharpened some longing she had successfully dulled.

And holding the baby had made her aware that the longing she felt for Lancaster, despite her betrayal by Troy, had not gone anywhere, and would never go anywhere.

The simple fact was she wanted Lancaster to be more in her life. Substantially more.

Sophie felt furious with herself as she stormed out the door. Had her experiences with Troy not taught her anything?

She was pretty sure that fury would carry her all the way back to the castle under her own steam!

Despite the labyrinth of twisting cobblestone streets, she knew which way to go: the castle, perched high on its cliff, loomed large over the entire village. She sighted it and headed that way.

She had not gone far when she heard footsteps coming behind her. Not running, but not going slow, either. She did not have to turn and look to know who it was.

"Sophie, come on."

She deliberately lengthened her stride.

"You just had to tell me if you were ready to leave," Lancaster said, his tone reasonable, but underneath it she could hear the definite edge of irritation.

"And pull you from your adoring fans?"

He was silent for a moment. "Are you feeling okay? Calum said you might not be well."

"I'm fine," she snapped.

"Are you angry?"

"No!"

"Come on, then, turn around. I'll drive you home."

Home. The place she didn't have. The place that baby had made her long for unreasonably. A place to call her own. People who loved her.

Whom was she kidding? Not just any *people.*

The *people* whom all the girls shared the same dream about.

"I'd prefer to walk."

"It's farther than you think."

"I don't care."

"You're a good twelve kilometers from the castle. Look, you already have blisters. Maybe it would be more sensible—"

She refused to give him the satisfaction of asking him how far twelve kilometers was in miles. Instead, even though her feet already hurt, Sophie gave him a withering look that let him know where he could put his sensibleness. He didn't say another word.

He walked her all the way back to the castle—and twelve kilometers was a long way. If he hadn't been there, she would have flagged down a cab partway, but with him walking stoically and silently beside her, pride prevented it even as her feet screamed their protest.

It started to rain. Her sweater began to feel like a wet clump of toilet tissue. She was pretty sure her feet were bleeding.

Lancaster did not say another word to her. He never even once mentioned that now he'd have to go back—or send someone else back—to retrieve the vehicle because of her stubbornness.

A reminder she was his job, and not a very

pleasant one at that. She tried, once, feebly, to remind herself what her mission for today had been.

Something about *his* happiness.

Sod that, a voice inside her said.

CHAPTER NINE

THERE WAS NOTHING on God's green earth, Lancaster thought, quite as indecipherable as a woman. Every other creature—including most men—was nearly completely predictable in its nature and patterns.

Sophie was angry.

So angry she was walking home despite the fact he was pretty sure her feet were causing her agony inside those shoes. The shoes were not made for walking, by the way, built like a pair of slippers.

Not that he was crazy enough to weigh in on that with her. The truth was, halfway there, when it was obvious to him that she was carrying on based on her stupid rather-die-than-admit-an-error stubbornness, he had to fight a desire to pick her up, throw her over his shoulder and carry her the remainder of the way.

With a man, Lancaster would be pleased that they were experiencing the natural consequences of a poor decision. With a man, he might reluctantly admire that level of stubbornness. But with Sophie, he found his feelings almost as indecipherable and as illogical as her behavior.

Pick her up and throw her over his shoulder? Picturing it gave him grave satisfaction, even as he recognized it as a primal desire, not the kind of thought he *ever* indulged in.

He turned his thoughts elsewhere. Why was she angry, exactly? He couldn't very well ask her, when she had denied being angry.

He cast about in his mind for something he might have said or done, but came up blank. Basically, he had barely seen her once they'd arrived at his aunt's house.

Was *that* it? He'd neglected her? It wasn't as if he was her date, and, in fact, he hadn't even wanted to go. For exactly the reason that had unfolded, thanks to her.

Swarmed by his well-meaning family. Children—some the same age as his son would have been—adoring him for no reason at all.

It pierced his preoccupation with the indecipherable woman beside him, that those children had not caused him pain this time.

It was a first.

And somehow, it felt as if he was not ready for that particular first—to not grieve his son in every baby he held, in every child's face that he saw.

And the girls, most of whom he'd known his entire life, all thinking they wanted to save him from *something*. A life of loneliness? His own company? His sadness? He hated that.

It started to rain, ever so lightly, and then harder. Her sweater was getting plastered to her. Since he had ruled out picking her up and throwing her over his shoulder, Lancaster shrugged off his jacket.

"Here. Take this." It was a command, not a request, but naturally Sophie was not going to be commanded.

"Quit being so coat-over-the-puddle chivalrous. It belongs to a different time. I'm fine."

She wouldn't think he was so chivalrous if she knew what he was thinking. What belonged to a different time was throwing her over his shoulder. He took a deep breath. He took his jacket and draped it lightly over her shoulders.

"You'll freeze," she said ungratefully.

"I'm used to hardship."

She cast him a look, and for a moment he

thought her curiosity had been piqued, but if it had, she resisted the temptation to ask him, which was *good* because, remembering how he had felt when she had taken his hand the other night, he did not want to be discussing the hardships of his life with her.

Finally, in the near dark, their journey completed in silence, they arrived at the palace door. He'd had twelve kilometers to think about it, but he found Sophie as indecipherable as when the trek had started. She was no quitter, though. He had to grudgingly give her that.

"You needn't worry about me tonight," she said, stiffly, taking his jacket off and handing it back to him. He was glad he had insisted: she was shivering despite having had it. "I won't be going out. At all. So you can go dry off—"

Her eyes lingered for a moment on the shirt that clung transparently to him, but then her nose went back in the air. "Or you can figure out what you're going to do about the car. Or whatever."

There was something about the way she said that—her casualness just a little too deliberate—that put him on red alert. He went from being a man who found all women—and one woman in particular—indecipherable, to being 100 percent pure soldier. Every soldier he'd ever known who was worth their salt had a "hinky" sense— a strange knowing when things were about to go down.

And so Lancaster knew that instead of going home, having a hot shower—or maybe a cold one, if he thought about her eyes on his wet shirt—and turning on the TV to watch a nice, uncomplicated, completely decipherable soccer game, he would be doing something else entirely.

He wished he'd eaten more at the *ceilidh*. And that he wasn't soaked to the skin. But he was not a man given to mourning wishes that did not come true.

"Have a good evening," he said smoothly, as if she hadn't alerted him at all.

He got it. He got it entirely. She wanted to go get rid of the chill, and soak those aching feet, and she wanted to do it in privacy.

So, she'd never even know he was there. He pulled his jacket back on. It provided zero warmth over his wet shirt, but it smelled tantalizingly of her.

He alerted the guard on the door, but then went and waited, scanning the wall of the castle for the ground-floor window he knew was hers. He watched the light go on, briefly, and then back off. The window creaked open, and she slid out it, backward, feeling carefully for the ground with one foot.

She found the ground, then turned and scanned the area. She did not see him, and she obviously thought he had taken her at her word. She was wearing a long raincoat, and had a bag in one hand, sneakers on her feet. The outfit looked like something a midnight peeper might wear. It was obvious she had not expected anyone to see her. She had a torch and she turned it on only when she was out of sight of the castle, and on the wooded path that led to the hot springs.

Sticking to the trees, Lancaster kept her in sight. It was obvious she was nervous out here by herself, and yet determined at the same time. The rain had dampened the leaves, and he moved soundlessly. It was ridiculously simple, given the circle of light that was illuminating the path in front of her.

He should, he thought, give her at least some rudimentary lessons in how to detect if she was being followed, and how to make it a whole lot less easy to follow her.

However, wouldn't that just be making his job

more difficult? Maybe before she left Havenhurst, when she was outside the circle of his protection, he would make sure she had the skills she needed to protect herself. Some rudimentary self-defense would be good, too.

But Lancaster was aware that he didn't like thinking of her leaving Havenhurst, and certainly not of her being outside the circle of his protection. This current threat to her would come and go, of that he was certain. But her proximity to the royal family would not change, and it seemed only a matter of time before another threat leaped up to take its place.

This was life's hardest lesson, one he seemed destined to repeat over and over again. Sometimes he was helpless to protect those he—

What? a voice asked him, its tone faintly mocking. Those you *what*?

Feeling things for people just made his life more complicated. Though, without warning, he was not sure how his life could become more complicated. The job of protecting Sophie went from simple to difficult in the blink of an eye.

Because she had entered the glade.

Havenhurst was covered in hot springs. Secret little grottos could be found all over the island.

And yet this one was special.

The pool was not large, not much bigger than the koi pond the queen loved. Two strokes would carry a good swimmer right across it.

But it was magical, especially on a night like this. Its own steam, combined with the darkness of the rainy night, created a sense of an enchanted place that a veil of fog was parting to reveal. The water of the springs danced with its own light, a light turquoise around the worn-smooth rocky edges, turning to pockets of indigo where the water was deeper.

The moist, warm air created an ideal environment for plants, and though no one knew how they had gotten here, exotic ferns and greenery that one expected to see only in the tropics dipped their fronds in the water and grew with lavish abundance.

Sophie paused on the edge of the water.

Lancaster ordered himself to turn around.

But in his head he could hear her saying, after he had assured her none of his guardsmen would ever sneak a peek, *They're just men.*

And it turned out, he was just a man, too. Because he did not turn around. He held his breath as the raincoat slid down off her shoulders.

Now who was the midnight peeper?

Was she naked under there? When she didn't know who might be in these woods watching her?

He felt furious at her lack of caution in the face of her own vulnerability.

And even more furious at his own vulnerability.

The raincoat slid down farther. He was appalled that he was not sure if he was thankful or disappointed that she had on a bathing suit, underneath. She stepped out of the puddle of the raincoat, and he saw it wasn't a bathing suit, at all.

It was one of those confections from Top Secret. Which begged the question: When had she gone back there?

Did it matter? This inability to turn away—to be so mesmerized by her beauty that he was powerless over himself—was proving he was a complete failure at his job. His perspective was gone. The shield of his professionalism had been broken. His walls had been breached. His mission—her protection—was as foggy as the night-darkened mist that swirled around the pool and around her.

Suddenly, he could not do this. The dishonesty of watching her when she did not know she was being watched grated on his sense of honor. It felt as if it would be a lie between them, forever, that he had watched her without her knowledge, and he could not bear it.

He stepped out of the shadows of the trees.

She caught the movement out of the corner of her eye, and turned slightly, tilting her head toward him.

Maybe he was not nearly as good at this job as he had given himself credit for, because if Sophie was surprised to see him, she did not let on. She did not scrabble to put her raincoat back on. She did not try to fold her arms over herself.

The whiteness of her body appeared illuminated against the backdrop of night and fog. She looked like a goddess, and Lancaster had never been more aware of his own mortality.

She did not speak, and neither did he.

She regarded him with calm interest, and then she turned her back to him, as though he were not there, and slipped into the turquoise waters of the pool. She swam out to the center, its deepest point, and then ducked her whole body under.

Then she resurfaced, her midnight-dark hair

as slick as an otter's skin, water streaming like mercury down the luscious curves of her body. Gracefully, like a dancer in a dream, she made her way through the pool and sat on a rock ledge submerged in the water. She closed her eyes and tilted her head back. And as if all that wasn't bad enough, temptation enough, then she stuck out her tongue, ever so slightly, to catch the rain that fell.

Lancaster frowned. Was he trembling?

Perhaps. He was hungry and he was wet. She knew he was here, now. He had done the honorable thing. He would fade back into the trees now. He would—

"Connal."

He froze, the sound of his name on her lips, again, felt like a benediction he had waited for without knowing he waited.

"Come get warm. I can see you shaking from here."

He could feel his frown deepen. She wasn't even looking at him. How could she possibly see him shaking? And yet, he was, and it was not exactly the manly impression he wanted to be making on her.

When had he started wanting to make any kind of impression on her?

"Do you have to be so strong, all the time?" she asked, still not looking at him, her face lifted to the rain that ran down it in silver droplets. Her tone as soft as a touch.

Yes, something in him cried out, but the word did not make it from his tormented mind to his lips.

"No," she answered for him. "Lay down your shield, Connal. Lay down your sword."

No, that voice within him cried.

"Come on," she said, her voice soothing, a voice a mother would use on a reluctant child. And at the very same time, the voice of pure seduction.

He could not get in that pool with her.

"Come," she said.

He would, he realized helplessly, do anything she asked him to do.

He would lay down his shield and his sword for her. He walked to the edge of the pool. With his eyes locked on hers, he shrugged out of his soaked jacket, peeled off the wet shirt underneath it. Slowly, aware of her eyes on him, his hand went to his belt. He undid it, and then his zipper. He expected to feel weak, giving in to temptation like this.

He was putting aside his job, what he'd been trained to do his entire life. He was giving himself over to the pleasure that the pool promised.

That Sophie's eyes promised.

He let the trousers drop, and stood before her in nothing but his boxers. Her eyes drank him in, darkening with unapologetic appreciation.

Connal Lancaster waited for that feeling he feared and hated the most to come over him. That feeling that happened when a man surrendered the only thing he really had. Control generally, and self-control, specifically.

Failure. He waited for it to wash over him, to remind him what a puny thing a man was in the face of larger forces.

Instead, standing there before her, her gaze unflinching on his near nakedness, Connal Lancaster felt something he had very rarely felt.

Freedom.

He dived cleanly into the shallow, turquoise waters.

CHAPTER TEN

"YOU SHOULDN'T HAVE come here by yourself."

Despite the softness in Lancaster's tone, it was so apparent to Sophie he was a man who was used to giving commands and accustomed to being obeyed.

Shouldn't have sounded like *shouldna* and it was impossibly sexy.

Lancaster was sitting on the rock ledge beside her, the water lapping at his powerful pectoral muscles and his broad chest. His eyes were closed and his head was tilted back, revealing the strong column of his neck, the jut of his Adam's apple. Water was dotted like tiny diamonds in the stubble of his whiskers, and in the thickness of his lashes. Sophie watched the raindrops slide down his perfect features and could, unfortunately, picture all too clearly her fingertips following their path.

"You said it would be good for my feet," she reminded him.

"That's not the part I've a problem with, lass."

Lass. His voice felt like a touch whispering along the back of her neck.

"I've never felt safer in my life than I do here on Havenhurst, Connal. It feels as if this is the land where nothing bad could ever happen."

She realized, instantly, what a terrible and insensitive thing that was to say. "I'm sorry," she said.

"Bad things happen everywhere. I think you know that."

"Wh-what do you mean?" she stammered.

"Has something happened to you?"

"I don't know what you mean."

"You have an exaggerated startle reflex. I've noticed it a couple of times. When that guy grabbed you on the way out of the pub the other night, you looked truly frightened. Did your fiancé do something to you?"

Sophie looked at him. His voice was measured, but there was a contained fury in him when he suggested that. He had noticed so much about her. There was also a feeling of being *seen* in a way she had not experienced before.

"He didn't hurt me physically, if that's what you're asking."

"I guess I'm asking who did."

She scanned his face, then sighed. He had told her so much about himself. Trusted her with it. Now, she felt as if she could trust him with one of her own secrets.

"When I was a little girl, my mother was attacked," she said, her voice catching. "My mom was born in Mountain Bend, the most beautiful girl in town. She won beauty contests—"

"Ah, so that's where you get it."

The admission that he found her beautiful somehow made this story even easier to tell.

"As silly as that seems now, she still has those banners on her dresser. My dad came to town as a mill manager, a university-educated office guy. As different from the local boys in Mountain Bend as night is to day. She fell hard for him, and left the guy she'd been going steady with cold. She married my dad, who ended up firing the old boyfriend for showing up to work at the mill drunk.

"My dad traveled a lot on mill business. One night, the old beau and some of his pals broke into our house. Well, not broke into exactly, because we never locked the doors before that. I was about six or seven at the time, and remember waking up to the sound of my mom screaming.

"By the time I got to the living room, my uncle Kettle was coming through the front door. We never found out how he knew there was trouble that night but he arrived, just in the nick of time, to save his baby sister.

"It's funny," Sophie said softly. "I have not thought of that for the longest time. But you're right. It's in me. Some kind of fear that never quite goes away. We never, ever talked about it."

"Maybe now that you have some of that fear will go away," he said, his voice unbelievably gentle.

And it felt like it might not because she had talked about it, though. Because she could *feel* his protection. Maybe, even as she grated against it, that was why she felt as safe as she ever had here on this island.

She had not been surprised to see Lancaster step out of the trees. Had she known he was there, as if, by some sixth sense she knew his proximity to her in the world?

"They're in bad shape, lass? Your feet?"

She was grateful for the change of subject. "Yes."

"You shouldn't have walked from the *ceilidh*."
Shouldna.

She sighed. "My life is probably just a long list of *shouldnas*." For some reason, she thought of Troy, and she saw her relationship with him in a new light.

I seem to go for a type, she had confessed to Lancaster the first day she had come back here.

Had a largely unacknowledged fear driven her toward a certain type of man? Men like her uncle who had saved her mother that night?

"You have no one to blame but yourself," he said, unsympathetically, obviously referring to her feet and not her heart. "Stubborn."

"Ah, something we agree on."

Wasn't Connal Lancaster also that type? Not really. Troy had been faintly arrogant in his gym-enhanced strength. Not quite a bully, but always on the lookout for opportunities to prove himself as stronger, faster, more fearless.

Which she, admittedly, had been drawn to.

Connal was different. A quiet strength, an unspoken confidence in his abilities, a man who would lay down his life to protect others.

He cast her a look that erased the jumble of thoughts—particularly about Troy—from her mind. Then he slid off the bench beside her, and stood in front of her.

Connal Lancaster was, without a doubt, the most beautifully made and natural man in the world. His skin was wet from the rain and the springs. Fog and steam swirled around him. Each muscle, each curve, each rib seemed as if it had been carved by a master artist from smooth, pure alabaster. He was Michelangelo's *David*. He was Bonnat's *Samson*. He was Conca's *Hercules*.

No wonder all the girls fawned after him, and dreamed their silly dreams of being the one. Sophie would not—

But then he reached into the water. With a tenderness that both shocked her and slayed her determination to not have any dreams at all about him, he cupped his hand under her calf, lifting her foot up through the steaming pool.

While Sophie was aware of her heart moving into the galloping rhythm of spoons played fast, Lancaster was purely a clinician. He frowned at the damage she had done, set that foot back in the water, and before her heart had any hope of slowing down, he picked up her other foot and inspected it.

He let it slide from his grasp, and she was not sure if she was relieved or let down by this reprieve from his touch. He turned from her, went to the pool's edge and braced both his arms against it, making the rock-hard edge of his triceps ripple and making her stomach drop dizzyingly, like a rock from a cliff. He lifted himself out of the pool with easy, fluid strength.

Sophie ordered herself to look at anything but him. But it was impossible. He had become everything, and she could not take her eyes off him. He fished through his pants pocket and came out with a small blade. He went to one of the shrubs that grew around the pool and sliced several leaves from it.

He came and lowered himself back into the water. "Sit that way," he said, motioning to her, "and stretch your legs out in front of you."

He was a man used to giving commands and being obeyed, and she found any desire she had to defy him had melted at his first touch.

She did as he asked her, and watched as he sliced the top of one of the plump leaves he held. It oozed some thick white liquid into his hand.

"Are you familiar with the aloe vera plant?"

She nodded.

"This plant is a cousin. Our ancient books speak of its healing powers."

It occurred to her what he intended to do. It occurred to her she should protest, or pull away. It occurred to her she was going to experience powerlessness as she had never quite experienced it before.

But Sophie could not speak as he again raised her left foot out of the water, cupping the heel in his hand. Her foot looked tiny in contrast to the strength and size of his hands. He bent his head over it, inspected it again, touching each of the blisters. His touch was unbelievably tender for such a powerful man. She remembered him holding the baby, Rowan, earlier, all that beautiful strength tempered. It was everything Sophie could do not to reach out and touch the wet, gold-red silk of his hair as he bent over her foot.

He began at her toes. There was a particularly nasty blister between her big toe and the second one, and he caressed the pain away with his touch and the thick ointment. Then he separated each of her toes in turn, and ran his oiled fingers between all of them, even those with no blisters. He worked with exquisite slowness, touching her lightly, as though he were stroking the wings of a butterfly. When he finished between her toes he worked the oil from the plant into each plump pad.

His touch, soft, sensual, exquisitely gentle, was making Sophie feel a tantalizing awareness of herself as a woman, and Lancaster as a man. That awareness screamed along her nerve endings, and was unlike anything she had ever experienced.

Without even glancing up—thank goodness, for what would be revealed in her face right now—he moved on from her toes. His grasp on her heel tightened marginally, and he slid his other hand over the top of her foot, his palm pressing deeply into her water-softened and warmed skin, sliding back, doing it again. And then again. And again. And again. As if there was no such thing as time. There were no blisters there. He knew it, and she knew it.

His touch lit some deep fire in the core of her being, and every stroke stoked it. It was the most exquisite of experiences, part pleasure and part pain. The pain was not physical, but it was like having a hunger that could not be satisfied, an intensifying thirst that could not be quenched.

He switched again, moving from the top of

her foot to the bottom of it. The slowness of his movements, as he kneaded deeply into the ball of her foot and the arch, was both exhilarating and excruciating. He moved to her ankle, and then to her calf. There were no blisters on her ankles, or her calves, either, and yet she was helpless to protest. Was he being deliberately so sensual?

Or did he just have a way about him? Being sensual was in every motion he made, every breath he took, every word he spoke. Being sensual was as natural to Lancaster as breathing.

Finally, when Sophie thought she could not take another second of what he was doing without doing something to slake her thirst and hunger for him, he surrendered her foot.

The relief—and the sense of loss—lasted seconds. He picked up her right one. And began the dance of touch all over again.

Sophie had to bite her lip to keep from moaning, and she had to make a conscious effort not to squirm. She closed her eyes and clutched her fists at her sides below the water against the tender torment of his touch.

Closing her eyes increased the intensity of feeling.

She knew, with a sudden primal knowing, that

there was going to be only one way to satiate her hunger. She had to have his lips. She had to taste him. She had to run her hands through the wet silk of his hair and over the hard plains of his body. She had to know every line of him. She had to celebrate his being a man.

She had to make him feel what he was making her feel.

And yet, a moment of sanity pierced the desire-driven thoughts.

It was just more of the same. Her history with Lancaster on endless repeat. Her *wanting*. Him resisting.

She was just like all those other girls who threw themselves at him, who wanted to penetrate his great mystery, who believed that the intensity of his masculine mystique could resolve some burning need in themselves.

How was she any different from any of them? Maybe she was worse, spending her life looking for someone to make her feel safe.

She yanked her foot out of his hand, and opened her eyes. He did not look the least surprised, as if he, too, had felt something dangerous building, had wondered if she would put an end to it.

He was looking at her, something veiled in his eyes. *Her move.* Why had he done this to her, given her history with him? Did some part of him enjoy her weakness?

But it was going to be a different move this time. She scrambled from the pool, before she gave in to the temptation. She was aware of his eyes on her, but when she glanced back, his gaze was hooded. Did he not feel any of the red-hot desire that was threatening to burn her up?

"I'm overheated," she said. *And how.* She glanced down at herself. The delicate underwear had become transparent. For a moment, she just wanted to hide herself, but then she wanted something else more.

To make him feel the helpless sense of desire he had just made her feel. To make him suffer as she was suffering. She stood there, letting the water slide down her body, unflinching from his gaze.

But if he was in any way tormented, it did not show. Instead, he broke the eye contact between them, lifted himself from the pool, turned his broad back to her, and began to pull his clothes over his wet body.

She could offer to share her towel. No, she

could not! She toweled off quickly, threw her raincoat on, jammed her feet back in her sneakers and headed for the pathway.

How could she make him see she was not the same as every other woman in his world? And how could she ever know if her attraction to him was just rooted in a long-ago incident, never truly resolved?

It came to her suddenly.

There was a secret about her Lancaster did not know. They had common ground. Something that they shared.

She noticed the rain had stopped, and the stars were beginning to shine through the trees, through the wisps of clouds. The world had a scent to it that was incredible, but, of course, all her senses were heightened right now.

"Better?" he asked.

Her feet! He was talking about her feet.

"Much better." She had never felt better and she had never felt worse. "Thank you. That was a lovely thing to do."

To torment a poor girl who has the hots for you.

But wasn't it time, really, to see if there was anything beyond that? If they had any common

ground beyond the chemistry he made her—
and a million others—feel? Wasn't it time to see
if she had grown beyond that childish need for
protection?

"I'd like to go fishing with you," Sophie said.
The path had narrowed and he followed behind
her. She glanced back at him.

"What?" He laughed. "Females don't fish."

Doona.

Sophie had to remind herself not to react with
aggravation. Havenhurst was not America. People here played more traditional roles, and did
not seem any the less happy for it.

"That's what you and Edward said about diving to Maddie," she reminded him. "And look at
her now." Of course, Sophie already knew how
to fish. Her quiet, bookish father had been the
most devoted and skilled fly fisherman in Mountain Bend. And she had been tagging along with
him since she was barely able to walk.

But she'd surprise Connal with that.

Or maybe not. Because from the look on his
face, he was going to refuse her this. Fishing
was, from what Calum had said, Connal's private
sanctuary, the place that had saved him when he
had refused all other comforts.

He would not want to invite someone into this most personal of his spaces. He would not want to invite her into his world.

She could tell already that he might have regretted joining her in the hot spring, that in his mind, some professional line had been crossed.

"Don't worry if you don't want to," Sophie said lightly. "I'll ask someone else."

She glanced back again. Bull's-eye! He *hated* that.

"You want to try it that badly?" he asked skeptically.

"I do."

Oh! If there were words one should ever avoid completely around a man who could turn you into a quivering bowl of jelly with just his touch, it was those ones.

I do.

Time, she told herself firmly, to find out if there was anything else here beside the leap of her heart and the sizzle of her blood anytime that he was near her. Time to find out if there was anything beyond the crazy fantasy that seemed to endure, despite her life experiences, despite her maturity, despite her admonishing herself not to invest any more time or energy in this vision.

And the vision was of her walking down an aisle, in a flowing white gown.

Toward him.

It was time to find out if there was any substance to this wisp of a dream that would not seem to let go of her no matter how hard she tried to break from its grasp.

CHAPTER ELEVEN

THREE DAYS LATER Lancaster scrambled over a slippery rock and turned to help Sophie. But this was what he needed to remember about her: despite that veneer of sophistication she now had, she was still a young woman who had been born and raised in wild country not unlike what he was taking her through.

They were following a trickle of a brook through a narrow, deeply shaded canyon. There was a bit of a trail, neglected, and covered in slick, fallen leaves. It was obstructed, regularly, by toppled trees and huge boulders.

Many other people, including men, might have decided at the first creek crossing that a day's fishing was not worth the fight through the rugged canyon.

But Sophie came over that rock with the agility of a mountain goat. She was breathing hard and laughing. He tucked his hand away before she even realized he'd offered it.

"Are your feet holding out okay?" he asked her.

She balanced on one leg, on the top of that slippery rock, and wagged a foot at him. It was clad in a sturdy hiking boot.

"Never better," she said.

One false move and she was going to topple a good six feet off that rock and probably keep going into the creek below.

He bit his tongue to keep from telling her to get both her feet underneath her. She was not one of his men to give orders to, and she would probably do handstands on top of that slippery surface to drive home that point to him.

She tucked the foot she had been wagging at him up against her thigh, creating a triangle. Then she stretched her hands way up over her head, pressed the palms together and drew them to her heart and closed her eyes.

She was doing yoga!

His breath caught in his throat at the contrast she had unwittingly created: feminine softness and suppleness against the hard, unyielding surface of the rock. Then, she wobbled, making him take a quick step toward her. Before he reached her, she let go of her pose and landed perfectly on both feet.

She couldn't be doing yoga on a fishing trip! The picture she had just created reminded him a little too strongly of her goddess qualities the other night. But again, if he said anything, she'd probably torment him with yoga poses for the rest of the day.

She smiled at him, and hopped down off the rock. To him, Sophie seemed at home in some way that she had not been since she arrived on Havenhurst. The deeper they moved into the woods away from the road, the happier she appeared, as if that super sophisticated outfit she had been wearing the day she got off the plane was a disguise, some sort of mask that hid who she really was.

But Sophie being who she really was, Lancaster told himself sternly, was not necessarily a good thing. Sophie was a beauty at any time. But, today, hair plaited in a thick braid, no makeup, a ball cap, sturdy boots, a pair of shapeless hiking pants and a plaid shirt, she looked better than ever.

Whom was he kidding? It had nothing to do with the wholesome mountain girl outfit she was looking so at ease in. It was the light that was on in her. Had something changed, ever so subtly, after she had told him about the attack on her mother when she was a child?

Whatever the cause, the goddess shone through, no matter what she was wearing. A man who had been cold too long could be drawn to that warmth, helplessly, like a moth to the brilliance of flame.

Just as he had been the other night. He was trying to banish the sensation of her foot in his hand from his brain. It represented the total collapse of his professionalism. And yet, even knowing better, here he was, testing himself again. He turned away from her and continued on.

Ten minutes later, the creek that the rough trail ran adjacent to cascaded down a series of mossy rocks into a pool. The canyon walls widened, and they emerged from its shadows. The sun filtered through fall foliage, golden. It danced across the dark waters of the pool, in a trail of starbursts.

"Oh," Sophie breathed, and stopped up short behind him.

He turned and looked at her. She knew. She recognized this as a place that was special.

He did not know how many other people on

Havenhurst knew about this place, but if they did, it was not because of him.

A fisherman's secret fishing hole was not something he shared with anyone.

And yet here she was, in his place, silent, looking about her with the reverence such a place deserved.

Lancaster knew he should have never agreed to take Sophie fishing. It was as close to sacred as anything came in his life.

And yet, after he had set her feet back down in that water the other night, he had felt like Samson without his hair. As if he was weak and no matter what she had asked him, he would have given it to her.

That was the real lesson of Samson—not that there were women out there waiting to betray men—but that love stole a man's strength from him.

Love.

Of course, he was under no illusions about love. What had sung through the air between him and Sophie was passion. A force of nature beyond reckoning with.

She was not young and untried, anymore. She was a woman who had been in the world, and experienced both the good and the bad it had to offer. That made everything more complicated.

And it was his own fault the chemistry between them had sizzled to life. What had he been thinking, revealing his presence at the hot springs to her? Dropping his clothes in front of her? Joining her in the water? What had he been thinking taking her delicate feet in his hands?

He had been thinking he was a hell of a lot stronger than he really was. Lancaster should be thankful she had asked for something as harmless as a fishing trip.

She could have asked him for what she had asked him for at Ryan's christening. He thought of that night, her beauty, the taste of her lips, how much he had wanted her. But not with a few drinks in her. If she had come back to him, the next day, and asked the same thing, he would have been in the same position he was in now. Not certain that he would be able to say no.

And how much more complicated his life would be if that is what she had asked for! So, why had he felt faintly disappointed by her request? For a fishing trip, instead of kisses? One was complicated, the other was not.

Though really? He was not at all sure about that now.

Because Sophie was standing on the banks of his favorite fishing spot, and it seemed complicated, indeed, as if she had invaded something that up until this point had been his and his alone.

He had carried the poles and the gear and now he set them down, focusing furiously on them, threading the poles, selecting flies.

Out of the corner of his eye, he watched as she went and stood on a large flat stone that protruded out over the deepest part of the hole. She was squinting down into it, almost as if she knew where fish would congregate.

He put on his fishing vest, and then took the fly-fishing rods over to where she stood. He joined her at the edge of the rock, and saw the dark shadows of fish in the water.

Normally, something would sigh within him. Today was different. He decided to get her set and then head a little farther down the pool, away from her.

He picked up his rod, felt the familiar weight of it in his hand. That familiarity felt as though it brought him home to himself, moved his focus in safe directions.

"I'll just show you."

It was as complicated and as simple as the dances the other night. It, too, had a disciplined rhythm to it, and he quickly fell into that, listening to the comforting song of his line hissing through the air in a nearly perfect snake pattern. The fly lit on the water, sprang away, lit again.

He could forget she was here, if he worked at it. But he glanced back at her. Sophie was watching him closely, but he knew she would not get it from watching. He could let her just muck about by herself, of course. Aside from the loss of a few flies, and some tangled line, what would be the harm in that? Untangling line could keep her occupied for the rest of the day!

But suddenly, self-protection aside, he wanted her to know this feeling.

The line singing, the sense of connection with all things, the moving to a rhythm so powerful it ordered the universe.

"Bring that other rod, and come here, lass."

He showed her again, this time with her standing right beside him.

"Now you try it."

She hesitated and looked at her rod, faintly perplexed. Lancaster changed his position so that he was standing behind her. He reached around her, and laid his arms the length of her arms, put his hands on her hands. She rocked back into his chest.

They had been here seconds, and he was touching her again! He had vowed, after the footsie thing at the hot springs, there would be no touching on this excursion. Unless it was an emergency, like her toppling off a rock because she was doing yoga in a place where she shouldn't have been doing yoga.

And yet, here he was, with her in no mortal danger at all, and his chin was just above the silky dark hair of her head, and the sweet curve of her back was pressed into his chest, and the scent of her was tickling his nostrils and obliterating the scents of clean water and fall leaves.

He tried to guide her through her first cast. It was a disaster, because she wasn't relaxing. The line dribbling out across the water instead of singing above it.

"Relax," he told her.

But she didn't relax. She was so tense her shoulders were shaking. Or maybe she was cold.

"Did you get your feet wet crossing that creek? Are you cold?"

"N-no."

He went very still. He ducked out from behind her and looked at her.

As he had suspected, she was laughing.

"This is why women don't fish," he told her sternly. "There's no giggling in fishing."

"I'm sorry," she said, very contritely.

He moved behind her, and tried to guide her through it again. Same thing. Laughing silently. Her shoulders shaking with mirth.

"This is serious business," he warned her.

"I can't do it," she said.

"You're giving up?" he said, astonished. Sophie did not give up! Look at that epic walk from the christening. "You haven't even tried it yet."

She turned and looked at him, almost with sympathy.

"I can't lie to you. That's what I can't do."

He tilted his head at her, baffled.

"I've been fly-fishing since I could walk, Lancaster. I'm probably better at it than you."

I can't lie to you.

It was the same thing he had felt when he had come out of the trees at the hot springs the other night. As if there could be no deceit between them, as if that was written in the stars somewhere.

Written in the bloody stars?

He decided he'd better focus on things other than what was written in the stars for them. Sophie thought she might be better at this than him? She couldn't possibly be serious. That was what he needed to be setting straight.

He came out from behind her, rocked back on his heels, regarded her with narrowed eyes.

"Show me what you've got, then," he invited her.

She looked carefully at the fly he had attached to her line. It was when she used a bit of spit to adjust it marginally that it occurred to him she wasn't kidding.

Then she turned away from him, and the line sang out of her rod. Her rhythm and her style were absolute perfection. Watching her was poetry.

She turned and looked at him over her shoulder. She winked.

He said a word under his breath that he rarely said.

"A small wager?" she suggested.

He glared at her.

"First one to get a fish wins."

"Wins what?" he asked.

Her eyes trailed to his lips. He was positive of that. Well, that didn't have any place in fishing, either!

"How about a piggyback ride over that first creek crossing near where we parked?"

"You're pretty sure you're going to win, since you can't piggyback me," he said.

"I could. In a pinch."

"You couldn't."

"Moot point, anyway," Sophie told him. And then she turned her back to him and put that fly precisely over the ledge, in the shadow where the fish loved to hang out.

Without asking, she had taken the best spot. Grumbling slightly, he headed downstream from her.

He hadn't even completed his first cast when he heard her gleeful shout. He glanced at her and saw the fish flashing at the end of her line. As he watched, she landed it perfectly, removed the hook, considered it and then let it go.

"That's your supper you just put back," he

warned her, glumly aware he had just lost the bet with her.

"There's plenty out there. I won't keep the babies."

Which meant he was honor bound not to keep the "babies," either. And they were the best tasting!

"You want to go double or nothing?" she called, giddy with confidence.

"You should just take your piggyback ride and be happy."

"Biggest fish of the day," she challenged him. "If you get it, cancel the piggyback ride. If I get it, you have to carry me over the two rough spots in the canyon."

Really? He had no choice but to take her bet. When he thought about it, he had to get out of that piggyback ride thing. If he'd thought there was any chance of her winning, he would have never agreed to such silliness in the first place. The thought of her clinging like a limpet to his back, her long legs wrapped around him, her laughter in his ear, was great incentive.

Lancaster had been fishing with his grandfather since he was just a wee lad. He had become very serious about it when he was a teenager.

But he had never experienced fishing like this. It had always been for him a place of deep solitude, of connection to nature, a place where he was totally immersed in the moment, no thought, no worry, no guilt.

It was not linked in his mind, except maybe in those long-ago days with his grandfather, to companionship. But today fishing became something else.

Fun.

Competitive.

Laughter-filled.

He had a feeling that given an opportunity, Sophie could take all things that a man was familiar with and edge them with light, make them feel brand-new again. She would make things he had been doing his entire life feel as if he had never done them before.

He'd landed quite a big fish, when a shadow fell over him. Startled, he looked up to see a cloud boil up over the edge of the canyon, blocking out the ray of sunshine that always seemed to illuminate this pool.

The problem with a woman like Sophie, he

told himself, quickly gathering his gear, was that a man ended up paying attention to all the wrong things.

He leaped over the rocks to where she was casting.

"Pack her up," he said, "we have to go."

"I do not have the biggest fish yet," she said, ignoring him.

He wasn't used to being challenged, and in these circumstances, it was imperative that he make her see he was the leader and there was room for only one.

"Sophie, the weather's changing. It can change very fast here. We need to get out of this canyon."

She scanned his face. "You're not just saying that because you have the biggest fish?"

He shook his head. The first drop of rain hit him. He turned from her and began to throw together their gear. He needed her to sense the urgency of this situation without making her afraid.

But the truth was that this particular canyon was susceptible to flash floods.

If he was by himself, he would take his ability to handle whatever nature threw at him in stride.

But he felt the enormous weight of being responsible for her, and not in a professional way, either.

He felt a man's basic need to protect a woman, yes, but he felt a shiver of awareness that it was becoming something even more than that.

CHAPTER TWELVE

SOPHIE HAD GROWN up in the mountains of Oregon. Weather there, as here, could change in a hair and be unpredictable. Still, nothing in her life experience had prepared her for the ferocity and suddenness of the storm that caught them as they made their way out of the canyon.

It had been a gorgeous fall day, the weather crisp and bright.

Now, they were caught in the middle of a storm worthy of winter: rain quickly turned to sleet, and made the path they had come in on slick and dangerous. The creek that gurgled beside the path was beginning to roar with faint menace.

It occurred to Sophie that perhaps she should feel utterly and completely terrified. She could barely see, her feet kept sliding out from under her and the wind was hurling ice at her with howling satisfaction.

And perhaps if she had been with anyone else

besides Connal Lancaster, she would have been terrified.

But his great confidence and his great strength never flagged. She watched him turn, in the blink of an eye, from the content man who had fished at the pool into a 100 percent battle-ready warrior. When she lost her footing on the treacherous path, he was always there, making sure she didn't tumble off an embankment or hit the ground. In more open places, he put his body between her and the worst of the storm, sheltering her. He was urging her on, but his voice was calm and sure, like a beacon of light a sailor might follow through a storm.

Instead of feeling overwhelmed by how long it was taking them to make the trip back to the car, instead of feeling the discomfort of getting wetter and wetter, she seemed to be operating on some kind of adrenaline rush. Sophie found herself faintly exhilarated, as if it was an adventure she was sharing with him.

Finally, they stood on the bank of the creek they had crossed this morning. Sophie felt the first niggle of real fear pierce the adrenaline. Just hours ago, the creek had been a trickle, postcard perfect, gurgling pleasantly over rocks. Now, it raged, thundercloud gray, its waters churning up debris from the bottom.

Lancaster dropped the rods and other items he had been carrying. He got down on one knee, his one arm steadying him.

"Get on."

"But I didn't win the bet," she said, pretending she was being defiant, and not what she really was, which was afraid. "You got the biggest fish."

"Sophie," he said, she suspected seeing right through her, something dangerous in his tone, "now is not the time. Get on."

She looked at the raging water and realized she had no hope of crossing it on her own. It wasn't particularly wide or deep—maybe six or eight feet to get across it, and maybe two feet deep—but it was moving horrendously fast. He was strong, she knew that, but even so something like panic tickled along her spine. Surely not even Lancaster could pit himself against an obstacle like this and come out the winner?

If he lost his footing, they could both be swept away.

On the other hand, what option did they have?

They had no shelter here. The warmth of the car was seconds away.

"Get on!" he said to her, and it snapped her out of her hesitation. She clambered on his back, and he rose, his arms closing tightly around her legs, and she wrapped her own arms around his neck.

He plunged unhesitatingly into the water. With each step, he battled to find his footing. She could feel his weight shifting underneath her, his enormous strength being used entirely, his muscles bunching, relaxing, bunching again.

He crossed the creek in less than two minutes, then set her down. Shocked, she watched him whirl around and head back into the raging water.

"Stop it," she screamed at him, over the roar of the water. They were safe! The car was right here! What was he doing?

He glanced back at her, but kept going. She shrieked at him again, pure panic rising in her. He made it safely to the other bank and filled up his arms with their gear. He was risking his life to retrieve *stuff*?

When she saw him come back across, saw how close he was to losing his footing and being swept away, her fear for him was replaced with fury, particularly once he was safely back on shore.

"How could you?" she yelled at him.

"I wasn't leaving my fishing gear," he said with not a trace of apology.

He was not hearing her! He could have been killed. Her helpless fury poured out of her, and she pummeled him with her fists.

He grabbed her wrists and held them tight, and even her fury was no match for the pure power of him.

"Tell me when you're ready to stop, and I'll let you go," he said, his voice aggravatingly calm, as if she was a child having a tantrum.

"You stupid ass! I can't believe you risked your life for worthless *stuff*." She tried to yank her hands free of him so that she could hit him again!

"That fishing rod was given into my keeping by my grandfather."

"And that makes it worth risking your life for?"

"Yes," he said firmly.

The fight went out of her and he let her go.

"You scared me," she whispered.

"I can't be something I'm not so that you won't

be scared," he told her with soft firmness. "I promised my grandfather I would look after that rod. It was the only thing he ever had of value."

She wanted, desperately, to tell him how dumb that was, but she could see *honor* was everything to him. When he made a vow, he would keep it.

I do, whispered along her spine, but she shook it off. She turned and walked toward the car. She admired what he had just done. And hated it. She loved him. And despised how weak that love had made her feel when he had crossed back over the creek to retrieve his precious fishing gear.

She loved him?

Sophie, she told herself, *you are supposed to be getting over that.*

Or, a small voice whispered, *seeing if there is any hope.*

There was no hope for loving a man who would put the well-being of his fishing rod above her feelings.

As she sat in the car, shivering, he packed their stuff into the trunk. He seemed to take his time about it, too. At least she was out of the driving wind and sleet. When he finally got in, she could see he was soaked to the skin. He left his door open, started the car and turned the heater on high. He sat sideways on the seat, and took off his boots.

He emptied what seemed to be a quart of water out of each one.

He had carried her across that creek, she reminded herself.

But, just in case it caused weakness, she also told herself it only meant she was at least as valuable to him as his stupid fishing rod. As she watched him wrestle his wet socks back onto his feet, she realized her own feet were so wet and cold they were losing feeling.

For the first time since she had known him, Sophie could not wait to get away from him. Maybe she would leave Havenhurst altogether. She loved Maddie. And Ryan. And Edward. But she wasn't really needed here. And staying was just proving too hard. A roller-coaster ride of emotion. It had been so much fun spending time with him this afternoon. Hopes up. He had not listened to her when she most needed him to listen. Hopes dashed.

Hopes up. Hopes dashed. The pattern of her entire history with this aggravating man.

She needed to be getting *her* life back on track.

She needed to be applying for a new job, not hiding from her failures here with a fake job. She needed to be thinking of how she went for the protector type, over and over again, and then was disappointed by them. She could learn to protect herself! She could take self-defense!

She needed to get away from Connal Lancaster. He didn't help her think straight. The opposite. How could any woman ever make a rational decision within a hundred-mile radius of the man?

A woman who had just experienced the disappointment of a fishing rod chosen over her sense of well-being could make a rational decision.

When they got back to the palace, she was leaving. As soon as it was humanly possible, she was leaving Havenhurst.

Except by now if there was one thing Sophie should have known it was this: every time she made a plan, whether it was to get married, or get her life back on track, the universe was determined to have the last laugh.

The weather outside was so bad that Lancaster was leaning forward, a grim look on his face as he tried to see beyond the swirling sleet. It kept jamming up the windshield wipers and icing the windshield. He had to stop and get out of the vehicle several times to clear the ice. She was not sure how he found it in himself to reenter the storm.

Now that she had made her decision, and now that the car was pumping out warmth, Sophie felt suddenly exhausted. Beyond exhausted.

She closed her eyes.

And was nearly thrown into the windshield when Lancaster slammed on the brakes.

"Sorry," he said, and then got out of the car.

Now he said sorry! She watched him fight his way through the wind and sleet. In the faint illumination of the headlights, she saw him staring at something.

Good grief, had he hit something? Someone?

Despite how she wanted to stay in its warmth, Sophie scrambled out of the car, too. She went and stood beside him. Her mouth fell open.

Where there had been a quaint little bridge over a sweet little brook this morning, now there was a pile of debris shoved up on the bank like so many toothpicks, the raging water sweeping by them.

She didn't know how he had seen it in time to

stop. They could have been killed. Again. His saving her life, for at least the second time today, made her attitude toward him soften slightly.

Slightly.

"Now what?" she asked him. "Do you have a phone?"

He nodded.

She waited for him to pull it out and use it. When he didn't, she wondered if it was because he knew the service would be spotty in such a remote part of Havenhurst.

But, of course, that wasn't the reason, at all.

"I don't want to make our rescue a priority," he said. "There will be people in far more need than us after a storm like this."

I need to get away from you would not count as a priority in his book Sophie knew, as he had shown her feelings barely rated on his radar.

He took his phone out and looked at it, before shoving it back in his pocket, away from the weather.

"No signal, here, anyway. I'll check in later. I'll have to watch the battery life."

"You can charge it in the car," she suggested, quite pleased with her contribution to their survival strategy.

"Normally, I'd say we should stay with the car, but all of Havenhurst will be digging out from under this storm. It could be days before they get to us." He looked at a sky darkening as night approached and made a decision. "Luckily, there's a little cabin not far from here."

Sophie felt something in herself go very still.

Just when she had decided there was absolutely no hope for her and Lancaster—not ever—she was going to have to spend days in a cabin with him?

It really was a cruel, cruel world.

He gathered anything he thought would be useful from the trunk, including the basket of freshly caught fish, and gave her *that* look when she offered to carry some of it.

Later, she realized how wise *that* look had been. Because the cabin was farther away than he had let on. She was starving, exhausted, soaked and thoroughly frozen. She could not have managed to carry gear as well as her weary self.

And then, just when she wanted to sit down beside it and weep—never mind impressing Lancaster with her newfound determination to look after herself—the path opened into a clearing. Even in the state she was in, and even in the horrible, dismal weather, she could see the cabin was an enchantment: whitewashed, roughhewn logs, turquoise shutters, a thatched roof.

"How long did it take us to get here?" she asked. "It felt like an hour."

"About eighteen minutes." He didn't check his phone for accuracy. If she wasn't so completely done, she might argue the point with him.

He opened the door, stood back and let her pass him. Sophie stumbled through it, and stood there, exhausted and shivering and wanting to weep. The cabin was uninhabited. And primitive. It was obvious there was no power. Why had she hoped for warmth?

He moved by her, fell on his knees before a stone hearth and shoveled kindling in. She saw the loveliest stack of dry logs beside it and went to stand in the meager warmth.

"You need to get out of those clothes," he said to her, without looking up when her shadow fell over him. It definitely was not a request. It was an order.

She stood there, dripping on the floor, her

mind moving ever so slowly. Get out of those clothes and into what?

He got the fire going, moved through the cabin, familiar with its layout. He came and stood before her, a rough blanket in his hands.

"Get out of those clothes," he said again.

Despite how utterly done she felt, she mustered a bit of pride. She folded her arms over herself and glared at him mutinously.

"Don't make me ask you again, Sophie." His voice was dark with warning that made her shiver more than her soaked clothes.

She grabbed the blanket out of his hand, planning on just pulling it around her soaking-wet clothes. He read her intent instantly, and stopped her with a look.

"I could only find one blanket, so don't even think of getting it wet," he warned her. "Naked. Now."

The words made her shiver harder. It wasn't as if he had designs, other than keeping her alive. She was going to have to concede. It was no different from being caught in her wet underwear at the hot springs. Only it felt so different. She had felt some semblance of control there.

"Somehow," she said, with a toss of her wet

hair, "I never pictured this particular moment going quite like this."

"Neither did I," he said, so softly she was not sure she had heard him correctly.

CHAPTER THIRTEEN

WHY HAD HE said *that*? Lancaster asked himself. The last thing Sophie ever needed to know was that he might have indulged the terrible weakness of imagining them together in any way, never mind *that* way.

Now she knew. They had *both* pictured this moment.

Of taking their clothes off.

And not at a hot springs, either.

For each other.

Thankfully, he had no time to indulge in weaknesses. He wasn't romancing her. He was taking charge in a situation that was probably far more dangerous than she realized. He estimated they were both on the verge of textbook cases of hypothermia.

There was no use second-guessing his choice to leave the vehicle. He had underestimated the time it would take to get here, because by himself he could have gone faster, eating up the ground with his long stride.

Sophie had already used up most of her resources getting out of the canyon, and her terror at his crossing back over the creek against her instructions had sucked up way too much of her energy.

Which made it even more imperative that she see there was room for only one leader in a situation like the one they were in, and it wasn't going to be her.

Mentally he ticked off his priorities, none having anything to do with her sudden modesty, modesty that had been nowhere in sight the other night at the hot spring.

Because, he told himself sternly, both of them had known there was an escape hatch that night, room to walk away. That was a luxury they did not have this time around.

He needed to get that fire going, get them both warm and dry and get something hot into them.

Out of the corner of his eye, he watched Sophie as she dropped the blanket at her feet. She managed to undo the laces on her boots and kick them off, but she was fumbling terribly. Her hands were so cold and shaky she couldn't get the buttons of the shirt undone. She was going to go into full-blown hypothermia before she managed to get her clothes off.

He took a deep breath, strode over to her, grabbed both sides of the front of her blouse in his hands and tore it open, buttons flying.

"I love it when you're masterful," she said through chattering teeth.

At least she hadn't said that this wasn't quite as she'd pictured it. He couldn't help but smile—inwardly, not outwardly—at her brave attempt to inject a bit of humor into her situation.

He quickly crouched in front of her, dispensed with the button on the front of her slacks the same way, and yanked the pants down. His hands brushed the flesh of her thigh and it was like a block of frozen ice.

Moving quickly, he rose again, reached behind her and dispensed with the soaked bra with one flick of his index finger. She glared at him and scrambled to cross her arms over herself.

"It seems as if you might have done that once or twice before," she said.

"Well, watch this, then, lass." He hooked his thumbs on either side of her soaked panties and yanked them down.

"Yes, you definitely have experience at separating a woman from her underthings. You might need a bit of work in the finesse department. On the panty part, anyway."

"Hard to get it right with my eyes closed."

"Your eyes were closed?" she asked.

Mostly.

"Thank you for saving my dignity." While she stepped clumsily out of them, he scooped the blanket that was at her feet and wrapped it around her tight, as if she was a sausage.

"See how painless that was?" he told her. "Hardly time to sneak a peek."

He wasn't sure if she looked relieved, or offended!

It was one of those rough wool blankets, the weave coarse, and he was sure it would feel scratchy and unpleasant against her skin, the delicacy of which he was newly aware of.

"You aren't going to like this," he warned her. Starting at her legs, he worked his way up, rubbing the blanket, hard, against her. She whimpered. "That hurts. It's not like when you did my feet."

"No," he agreed, "it's not like that at all. I'm sorry, lass. It can't be helped."

"What a letdown," she said. "Despite your efficiency at getting clothes off, you suck at foreplay."

It was something a man less disciplined than himself might take as a challenge. Ignoring her whimpering and his own wayward thoughts, he methodically rubbed the circulation back into her.

Satisfied that her shaking was subsiding, he pulled an old overstuffed sofa as close to the fire as he dared and set her down on it. Then he went and searched the cupboards, coming up with an ancient bottle of brandy. Her arms were pinned inside the blanket.

"Open your mouth."

"After the horrible attempt at foreplay, you're going to get me drunk?" she asked, but she opened her mouth.

He poured a shot of brandy down her throat and then took one himself.

"I am starting to believe I might live," she decided.

"No one dies on my watch." As soon as it was out of his mouth, he realized the enormity of that lie. He quickly gathered her clothes and began to pin them on a line that ran beside the chimney.

Sophie was watching him closely.

"I think it's your turn to dispense with your clothes, Connal Lancaster."

He turned and looked at her. She was right. He was cold to the core, and he could not be of any assistance to her if he got sick. He knew a man's strength was a puny thing against the ravages of being cold and wet. As a soldier, he had been taught there was hardly a worse enemy than that.

Still, he felt the surrender of it, as he reached for his buttons. He did not turn away from her.

"Somehow," he said, trying to tease her, and not quite pulling it off, "I never pictured this particular moment going quite like this."

He shucked off his clothes, felt instantly warmer without their wetness clinging to him. She averted her eyes when he freed himself of the wet boxers. He left the clothes in a pile as she managed to squirm free from a corner of the blanket, and she held it open to him. He hesitated for only a moment before climbing under there with her, pulling the coarse blanket tight around them again.

"Are you completely unclothed?" she asked him, her voice a squeak.

"As the day I was born."

She contemplated that.

"Hmm," she finally said, "this isn't quite as I imagined, either. It's about as romantic as cuddling up with a frozen ham."

"I'm no romantic, Sophie. I've disappointed others."

"Your wife and your baby didn't die on your watch," she told him softly, some intuition leading her directly to the heart of his every disappointment in himself. "It was a fire. You had no more control over that than over this storm. You told me you weren't even on the island when it happened."

He suddenly felt utterly exhausted. He could feel faint warmth creeping, with excruciating slowness, back into both their bodies. He could not fight, anymore, the need to tell her exactly how it had been, the need to dispel her illusions.

Maybe it was crucial in these circumstances. They were bound to bond to one another in this kind of survival mode, in this kind of forced proximity. He assumed they would be here days, not hours.

So, it suddenly felt imperative that Sophie know exactly who he was and how greatly he had failed the only time it had ever mattered.

"The regret," he said slowly, going somewhere he had gone only—but endlessly—in his own mind, "wasn't just that I failed to be there when I was most needed, it was that I was a failure as a husband. And a father."

"I don't believe that," she said stubbornly.

Her faith in him was troubling and undeserved.

"I didn't come from one of those big, happy families," he said. "My father was a career soldier, as I am. The Havenhurst forces are allied with other armies, and we share personnel, missions and assignments.

"My father was seconded for a mission to a place nothing in Havenhurst had prepared him for. He came back from his deployment minus an arm and a changed man. He refused to accept a disability pension, calling it charity.

"He was harsh, given to drink and episodes of violence. It was worse after my mother died. I was twelve. The only respite I had was my grandfather, who would take me fishing." He cast her a look. "I guess that's why his rod means so much to me. The only good legacy from my childhood. Anyway, I followed the lead of my three older brothers and left home as soon as the army would take me."

"I didn't know you had brothers."

So much she didn't know. So much he had succeeded at keeping from her. "They all serve overseas. We're not close. Survivors who bailed off that sinking ship as soon as we were able.

"My family became my brothers in arms in the guard. I loved my new life like a puppy who'd been kicked too often finally finding a good place to be. It wasn't just that I was fed and a life that had been utter chaos took on a soothing routine, it was that I started to hear words I'd never heard. *Well done. Brilliant. Good job.*"

He realized her hand was resting on the top of his wrist. When had she put it there? Why did he feel as if he was drawing strength from her, when in fact, the whole point of this story was to set up a barrier between them?

He wished he could shake off her touch, the comfort of her hand resting lightly atop his wrist, but his strength seemed to be waning.

"I don't tell you this out of disloyalty to my father," he said, "but to let you know there is nothing in my background that prepared me to be a family man.

"Not that that kept me from longing for what I had never had. When Ceyrah came along, she just seemed to love me so completely. I'd never had that before. But what started off as a blessing soon felt like a curse. She didn't like me out of her sight. She was bitter about my work obligations. She chaffed at every assignment I was sent on. She wanted me to love being with her, and love doing things with her, but I'm ashamed to say I was bored by every single thing she found interesting.

"I was a selfish bastard. I didn't know what to do with all that *need*. I was rising in the corps, and had been offered an opportunity to go to a military college off island. I wanted to focus on my career. She was opposed to me leaving, and there were no married quarters at the college. At twenty-one, I wanted a divorce, something that is almost unheard of on these islands. Her answer to that was to get pregnant. And I went off island anyway, leaving her to cope with the baby mostly on her own.

"People might say it's the wrong reason to stay married, but from the first moment I had held my baby in my arms, I felt what I had longed to feel my entire life. Needed. Complete. I loved him unreasonably when I was there. And he me.

His first word was *Da*, even though I'd been away for the majority of his life."

He stopped. He had talked too much. Perhaps more than he ever had. He pulled his wrist out from under her hand, and wearily rubbed his eyes, his whiskers.

He waited to feel crippled by the weakness he had just revealed, even as he knew it was necessary. He had done it for her own good. To help them both keep a distance from each other as whatever unfolded in this cabin unfolded.

Sophie was silent.

After a while she laid her head against his shoulder.

He felt something he didn't deserve to feel.

He felt her tolerance of him as the flawed man who he was. He felt from her something he had failed to give himself. Acceptance.

And instead of feeling weak and as though he had revealed too much—even if it was for both their sakes—he felt like a man who had carried a huge burden, a man who had not even realized the weight of what he carried until he had finally, finally set it down.

He slipped his arm over the sweet curve of

her bare shoulder. He kissed the silk of her hair where her head leaned against him.

He knew he should get up, tend the fire, clean and cook the fish. But he felt immobilized, unable to move. He told himself he'd do it in a moment.

"I forgive you," she said, her voice husky.

His failures, unfortunately, were not hers to forgive.

But then, before he delved too deeply into the topic he had forbidden himself, forgiveness, she clarified.

"For going back and getting the rod."

Feeling as light as he had felt in years, understood in some way he had never expected to be understood, Lancaster closed his eyes. He could feel that one shot of brandy burning in his belly. He let its warmth, and the fire, the sturdy walls of the cabin, Sophie's warming body, comfort him. He felt as if he was a warrior who had wandered endlessly, and finally, finally, finally found his way home. He slept.

CHAPTER FOURTEEN

SOPHIE WOKE TO THIN, watery light filtering through the cabin's two tiny windows. She felt warm and safe and she contemplated the richness of sensation inside her. It was more than contentment. Fulfillment.

Slowly it occurred to her she was not alone under the blanket. The warmth was emanating from the man beside her. She was buck naked and so was Lancaster.

Nothing with him would ever go as she imagined.

And yet, in some strange way, this was better than she imagined. She remembered his rich voice last night, telling her all of it.

Trusting her with all of him. His most deeply guarded secrets, the sense of guilt and failure he carried with him, more effective than a shield at protecting his wounded heart. Having him sleep so deeply beside her was a testament to what he had let go of.

She was cuddled into his side as he slept on his back. She tilted her head slightly, so that she could study him.

His hair, damp when he had climbed under that blanket with her, had dried adorably mussed. His eyelashes were so tangled and thick they cast a shadow on the upper part of that strong cheekbone. His face had roughened with red-gold whiskers overnight, and Sophie had to fight a strange longing to run her hand along their roughness, an intimacy that would belong to lovers, not people bound together by the ravages of the storm. The blanket had fallen away from his chest, and she watched the powerful rise and fall of the life force within him with reverence for what she was seeing.

Then she saw faint bruises darkening over the nipple of his left breast. She thought of how she had pummeled him with her fists in a fury of anger at him for going back across that raging creek. She was mortified. Really—with the exception of hitting Troy with the guitar—she was not like that!

Sophie was determined to make up for that lack of control.

She slipped from the bed, and found her clothes

where he had hung them. They were dry but they felt as if they had turned to cardboard. She put them on, nonetheless, aghast at the lack of buttons on her blouse.

She found his clothes, still in a wet heap, and hung them. She stole his knife and his belt, which on the very last hole, held her blouse shut and her pants up. She stoked the fire, adding kindling and blowing on the coals until the flames licked to life. It reminded her of her childhood growing up in a mountain village.

She opened the front door in search of the fish they had caught. The basket was still just outside the door, in nature's refrigerator. The storm was gone, though its remnants remained. The whole world was coated in a thin sheen of ice and it gave it a fairy-tale quality, as if every leaf and every blade of grass and every stone had been gilded in silver.

She stepped out into that fairy-tale world, took his knife and expertly cleaned the fish. This, too, reminded her of her childhood.

Back inside there were enough embers to take a cast-iron pan from where it hung on a hook in the rafters and put the fish in it.

"Ah," she heard his voice behind her, rough with sleep, say, "have I woken in heaven, then?"

Exactly how she had felt this morning!

"Did you clean them?" Naturally, being a man, he was talking about the fish.

"Of course I cleaned them."

"You didn't have to. I would have done it."

She didn't want him to feel she was his duty, someone to be looked after. She wanted to build on what had happened last night, and that would require this being a relationship of equals.

Relationship.

She said none of that to him. "Consider it amends," she said.

"For what?" He sat up, stretched mightily. He went to throw off the blanket and hastily re-thought it. "Would you pass my trousers?"

"They're still wet. I just hung them now."

He considered this, got up with the blanket around him, wrapped it around his waist and then draped it over his shoulder and tied a knot. "You are looking at the original kilt, lass."

She was indeed! She could barely drag her eyes away from the sight he made.

"It would help if I had my belt," he said, noticing it holding her ensemble together. "Otherwise I'm going to spend the whole day trying to keep this up."

"You should have thought of that when you were sending my buttons all over the place last night."

"Ah." His eyes went to her blouse and then skittered away. "What are you making amends for?"

"Look at your chest."

He glanced down, traced his fingers over the small bruises and looked back at her. "These little things? They don't hurt. It's my coloring that makes the slightest touch look as if I've been hit with a plank."

"Nonetheless," Sophie said, "I'm sorry for hitting you. It was a horrible thing to do. I've never done anything like that before."

"Except for a Fender over your ex's head."

She didn't know whether she was aggravated or flattered that he remembered every little thing she'd ever said to him.

He went over to the bench that acted as the entire kitchen, and rummaged around, turning back to her holding an old-fashioned perk coffeepot and a sack of coffee in one hand, and his makeshift kilt in the other. He held his finds up triumphantly.

"I'm really sorry," she said, again, feeling he was not getting her point.

He filled the pot, awkwardly one-handed, with water from a pump over a deep old enamel bowl that acted as a sink.

He came and crouched beside her at the fire. The most delicious man-in-the-morning scent mingled with the coffee grounds, tickled her nostrils.

"Let it go," he said easily. "It's a reaction to stress, lass, not a black mark on your character. It's not as if you could hurt me."

Her gaze went to the bruises.

"When we train men," he told her, "we deliberately test them with stress to see how they'll react."

"Did I fail the test?"

"I wasn't testing you," he said, sliding her a look. "At least not deliberately."

"That's not what I asked."

"Anger is not a bad reaction to stress. It needs to be channeled correctly, but I'd say, given the circumstances, you are holding up exceedingly well."

Sophie felt ridiculously pleased with his praise.

They sat on the warmed stone floor in front of the fire, and even though there were dishes and utensils, he suggested they might want to wait until they had been cleaned to use them as there were signs of mice in the cabin.

Instead, they ate the fish straight out of the pan, picking at it with their hands. Lancaster was as relaxed as she had ever seen him, as if some finely held tension had been let go last night when he had shared his secrets with her.

She was not quite as relaxed. In fact, Sophie wondered if she had ever seen anything as exquisitely sensual as Lancaster licking his fingers.

"I'm not sure I've ever tasted anything quite so delicious," she told him.

Or seen a man eat in a way that shook me to my core.

"Wait until you try the coffee." He carefully picked the perking pot out of the fire, plucked two enamel mugs from hooks that hung over the hearth and filled them.

It was true. She usually took both cream and sugar in her coffee, but she just sipped it the way it was. The coffee was incredible. Her eyes met his over the rim of the mug.

"Something about this kind of experience," he said, his tone soft and contemplative, "makes life feel so intense."

"Maybe the near-death thing?"

"We were never near death," he told her, as if she had insulted him.

"Maybe not, but still, something in me seems to be shouting, *I survived.* There is a sense of being alive and wanting to celebrate being alive this morning that is exquisite."

Probably, a little voice informed her, it had nothing to do with the survival experience and everything to do with waking up beside him.

Naked, the little voice insisted on reminding her, as if she needed reminding!

He looked at her. His eyes drifted to her lips, which she thought might be slightly glossed with fish oil, as were his. He looked quickly away, took a gulp of his coffee before setting the mug on the stones beside the fire.

"How about if you celebrate being alive by getting the kitchen in order, taking an inventory of what we have? I'll go in search of a cell phone signal."

"Aye, aye, mon captain."

"Major," he told her. He got up so abruptly his

kilt slipped. He grabbed it around his waist, and glared at her as if she had made it fall off!

"Whatever," she said to him. "Your dress is falling off."

"Dress?" he sputtered.

And then, he let go of whatever he was fighting, and their shared laughter was as glorious as the morning sun, filtered through the crystals of ice that hung everywhere, and pouring through the windows like liquid silver.

Suddenly, he seemed eager to get away from her, though, and he headed outside.

Sophie heated water, and found soap and filled the sink. She cleaned the counters first, and then washed every dish she could, stacking them to dry on every surface space. When she was finished, she looked at the jumble of the kitchen shelving system and organized it, making note of how much food there was.

She checked his clothes, and found them nearly dry. But dirty. She hesitated. Was she being nice or did she like seeing him in a kilt? She filled a bucket with soapy water and washed his clothes, rinsed them and rehung them by the fire.

Then she explored the cabin, and found sheets and made up the only bed. When she found extra blankets in bins under the bed, she realized one of them could sleep on the couch and one take the bed. But only if he knew there were extra blankets. Feeling exquisitely deceitful, as she heard him come in the door, she shoved the bins back under the bed.

She got up and, dusting off her knees, turned to look at him. He stood there like a chieftain, perfectly comfortable in his home-styled kilt. She saw he had found a rope, somewhere, and his rough garb was now cinched in place around his waist.

"There's enough food to last a month," she told him, "but only if you like canned haggis."

It occurred to her she was nesting. It occurred to her she *loved* the idea of a month here, with Connal, and one blanket, canned haggis notwithstanding.

No mention of those extra blankets. Or the fact his clothes had been nearly dry enough to put on, but now they weren't. Talk about playing with fire!

"We won't be a month," he said. "I had to walk quite a distance and find a knoll to get a signal on. Help is on the way. A blessing for you, because I can live on tinned haggis. I suspect you cannot."

"How long?" she said, feeling something sinking in her. Hours? Minutes? Days? She was very aware of what she was wanting.

"Hopefully, the guard will be here in two days."

And so once again, they hoped for different things. She wanted to play house, he wanted to get back to his duties.

Still, two days. Two whole days in total isolation with Connal Lancaster. She wanted to pursue the matter, like a tourist who had purchased a trip. What did two days mean, exactly? Two days and three nights? Forty-eight hours from this moment? But he had moved on.

"The palace can withstand almost anything, but it didn't have to. It, and the village, just caught the edges of the storm, but this part of the island was hit hard. The guard is in emergency mode, helping restore services and bridges as quickly as possible. It's part of what we train to do. These ice storms blow in off the Atlantic every year or two."

She could tell, even as she would treat those two days like an incredible gift, it chaffed him that he was not out there doing his part, the job he had been trained to do.

But she was not giving one second of this time to regret. She was staying in the moment. She was not, either, spoiling any of it with thoughts, like what did the future hold?

How did he feel about her?

How did she feel about him?

These few days were heaven-sent. An opportunity to do exactly what she had wished to do.

Get to know each other better, in the best possible way. Not on a *date*, those horrible awkward things where no one knew what to say, and way too much time was spent inwardly debating: *To end with a kiss? Not to end with a kiss?*

Which brought her to his lips again. And despite her vow to stay in the moment, Sophie found herself wondering how this day would end.

"I'm going to go outside and deal with firewood."

She began to suspect he was going to spend as much time trying to separate them as she was trying to bring them together.

"Hang on a sec, buddy. You can help me dry dishes first."

"'Tis women's work," he said.

"That's utterly ridiculous."

"It is?"

"You help me and then I'll come out and help you with the firewood."

"As if you would be any help with firewood."

"You need some educating, Major."

"Do I now?" He tilted his head at her, regarding this idea of teamwork—with her, anyway—as somewhat novel.

Then he shrugged, and she moved back into the kitchen, handed him one of the old flour sack tea towels she had found.

He took up that task of drying dishes and putting them away. How could he make such a routine domestic chore seem, well, sexy? And the sexiness didn't stop there, because, when they were done with the dishes, he rolled up his tea towel until it looked like a rope. There was mischief dancing in the green of his eyes.

"What are you—?"

"Just showing you it's a dangerous thing to let a man loose in the kitchen."

He snapped it at her behind. It missed, cracking in the air.

"Oh!" She ran, but the cabin was small, and

the couch became an obstacle that slowed her. He landed one and shouted with pure devilment at her exaggerated yelp of pain.

He cracked his towel at her again, and she shrieked with laughter and indignation, then turned to face him and began to roll her own towel into a lethal twist. She snapped it and it cracked in the air between them.

"Hey!" he said. He turned with pretended fear, his hands over his behind like a little kid afraid of a spanking, and ran. Unlike her, in his world there were no obstacles. He jumped over furniture and shoved things out of his way.

They chased each other around that little cabin until the rafters rang with their laughter, until they were breathless, until they were both covered in little red welts from where they had landed their shots.

He finally dropped his towel and raised both hands to her. "I surrender."

And she realized he *had* surrendered. She had seen Lancaster in many situations, and in many moods, but she had never seen him playful before. It felt like she had uncovered treasure.

He, on the other hand, seemed annoyed with himself. "It looks like the place has been ransacked," he said, dourly, going around and picking up overturned furniture, and setting it right.

"Enough fun and games," he said. "The real work begins. I can manage."

But she had a feeling he *wanted* to manage on his own, that he saw what had just occurred between them as a loss of his proverbial control.

"I'm coming."

Did he roll his eyes, before he stood back from the door and held it open for her? Outside, it was as if music played as ice melted and dripped from every surface. There was a stack of unsplit cordwood beside the cabin. Some of the rounds were two feet across.

"How are you planning on helping me with that?" he asked, raising an eyebrow at her.

It had a "Me Tarzan, you Jane" feel to it.

Of course, she could not split wood that size. But she had grown up dealing with firewood and there was always a job for everyone and for every level of strength. She went to the heap of wood, rolled the first one down, placed it on its end, so that it was standing up, ready for him to split. And then she did another, and another.

He realized what she was doing, and followed

the trail of standing logs she was leaving him as if it was a challenge, as if he needed to keep up to her.

Thunk.

Logically, Sophie knew it was the sound of the ax, swinging into those enormous rounds of wood, breaking them cleanly in two, but when she turned to look at him, her mouth went dry.

Connal Lancaster was the pure poetry of sheer masculinity as he pitted his strength against the timber. She wondered if there was a sight more incredible than watching a strong man, who knew what he was doing, splitting wood.

She watched him set up: legs apart, his whole body stretching upward as he lifted the ax over his head. Then, swinging, the bunching and rippling of arm and torso muscles as the blade took on the momentum of his strength, and followed its own weight down to cleave those huge rounds of wood in two as if they were matchsticks.

The makeshift kilt left most of his upper body unclothed, and so Sophie could really see the play of muscles, the fine sheen of sweat that began to make them look oiled.

Thunk.

She was pretty sure that was the sound of her own heart falling. Again. And again. And again, as he moved like a machine through that wood, splitting it cleanly and with seemingly no effort.

"I'm catching up to you," he warned her.

She was pretty sure he was as intensely aware of her watching as she was aware of him working. She turned from him, and upended more wood, but awareness tingled through her entire being.

The ancient dance was taking place between them. Is that why she had washed his clothes? Is that why he seemed to be delighting in showing her his enormous strength?

The world was supposed to be beyond all these primitive demonstrations of masculine and feminine roles.

So why did it feel so right? And so good?

She contemplated that *thunk*. Had she fallen in love with him? Possibly she had never fallen out of love with him, so *more* in love with him? What had Troy really been to her? A cheap substitute for this man? No wonder it had ended in bitter disappointment.

Contemplating loving Lancaster was too frightening. Maybe, Sophie told herself, she was just in love, for the first time in a long, long time, with every single sensation involved in the process of being alive.

CHAPTER FIFTEEN

"I THINK WE have enough wood," Sophie said. Lancaster split one more piece and leaned on the ax. He didn't want to appear as grateful for her calling a stop as he was. He'd been trying to keep up with her, competition leaping up between them as naturally as breathing.

He noticed a fine sheen of sweat had appeared over her upper lip, and in the hollow of her chest where the blouse pulled open, despite the belt, drawing his gaze. He looked quickly away to where she had been stacking that wood against the side of the cabin as fast as he could split it.

The competition had gotten away from him. There was enough wood there for a year's use, not two days. Somehow, he had just been enjoying it. Being together. Friendly competition, even as they worked as a team.

All right. Enjoying her lithe, sure movements. Lancaster admired her willingness to do hard work, her laughter, her little quips, her pausing to brush the hair, falling from her braid, back from her face.

And in those pauses, she would look at him, and he knew what he enjoyed the most: her awareness of him, the hungry way her gaze rested on his sweat-slicked muscles.

"I like to leave things better than I found them," he said, setting down the ax. He felt as if he had just finished a really hard workout. He felt as if he needed a shower. He felt as if he had better not say that in front of her at the moment, because she would probably figure out a way for him to clean up and it would probably involve nudity.

"I'll get us something to drink," she said. "Look. There's a swing on the porch. We can pretend we're old."

The sun had come out, and it was pleasantly warm despite the fact it was fall. He sat down on the porch swing. The ice was melted from the glade, and the moment felt full and peaceful. He imagined growing old with someone at his side.

Sophie came out balancing two glasses of water, and a box. She handed him his water, and sat beside him. The swing was small, barely built for two. Maybe for one and a half. Her leg and shoulder were touching his leg and shoulder.

She turned her head and sniffed him. "You smell good."

"In what way?" he asked. How could he smell good? He needed a shower.

She blushed ever so slightly. "You smell like a man."

Now that she mentioned it, she smelled good, too, the remains of some shampoo scent clinging to her hair, a sweet scent that seemed impossibly lovely after what he had just witnessed her doing.

She smelled like a woman.

"What is this?" she said, prying open the lid of the wooden box.

"It's a game that's popular here."

"Are all the parts there? Can you show me how to play?"

He tried to think when the last time he had played a game was. Maybe a boring night in the barracks, years ago?

She was looking at him hopefully.

Why not just play? There was nothing else that needed doing. Why not give himself over to an afternoon of frivolity?

He remembered when Maddie had taught Edward to play cards. They still played together. Lancaster came in on them sometimes in the middle of a poker hand. Maddie cheated and Edward loved it.

Lancaster suddenly felt a strange longing to have, even for one afternoon, what he had seen between the prince and the princess.

"Sure," he said. "I'll show you. Let's go in and set it up on the table."

As it turned out, Sophie was very quick to pick up the rules and the purpose of the game. She was also animated. And competitive. The day drifted into afternoon to the music of her laughter.

He checked his clothes partway through the afternoon, found them dry and put them on.

"Did you wash these?" he asked.

She actually blushed.

He didn't have the heart to tell her that she hadn't rinsed them well enough. He'd been cursed with the supersensitive skin of a redhead, and he would be breaking out in blotches in no time.

They ate tinned haggis as the day died. Or he ate it. She nibbled tentatively, making faces.

Without discussing it, with light fading, they did the dishes together after dinner. And then, stoking the fire with the wood they had cut together, they sat side by side on the couch.

The conversation was so easy between them. They talked first of mutual interests. She entertained him with a few tales of Prince Ryan. He told her about his first meeting with Edward.

"His grandfather sometimes fished with my grandfather. Not often, but sometimes. I think he longed to leave the formality of his life behind him, and liked to escape his entourage. He would show up, from time to time, unannounced. As far as I know, besides me, he is the only one my grandfather ever revealed his secret spots to.

"I was invited one day, because the king had a lad with him. I was quite young, maybe eight or nine? And the lad was younger. I think I was aware that the king was important, but maybe not aware of how important.

"Anyway, in my young mind whatever his importance was, it did not extend to his grandson, who was a bit too cheeky for my liking. I was doing my best to ignore him, when I saw that he had grown bored, opened the fishing kit and was throwing the flies my grandfather had made in the drink. Now, when I think about it, it was without malice, but at the time, seeing this well-dressed young upstart entertaining himself by carelessly throwing the flies my grandfather had worked so hard on in the water, I just saw red.

"I tackled him, and somehow we tumbled off the bank into the water. He likes to say, now, it was that day we both learned how to dive, and also the day I was introduced to my destiny. Even though it was my fault that he was in there, I managed to pull him back out before he drowned.

"My grandfather was appalled. It's the only time he ever cuffed my ears, but Edward's grandfather told him to stop, and laughed. He said Edward deserved it. And then he, the king, used his net and rescued all those flies from the water, treated them with such reverence. My grandfather gave them to him and he, that man who had everything, acted as though he had been given a treasure worth more than gold."

"Is it your destiny, Connal? Do you think you will protect Edward and his family forever, or do you have other ambitions?"

He glanced at her. The cabin was full dark, save for the flickering light of the fire. Sophie looked gorgeous. And she wanted to know him. And without warning, he wanted her to know him. He wanted her to know that he was a humble man, who lived simply, and whose definition of ambition would probably not match her own.

"I know *service* is not a popular term in a world driven by raw ambition, but in my world, I could ask for no greater honor than to serve that family and protect them. I feel it is what I was born to do. This is my ambition—to do what has been given to me with every bit of heart that I have."

Rather than seeing his ambition as humble, Sophie nodded as though he had confirmed something she already knew of him. He got the feeling she did not disapprove. She asked questions that led him into telling her about his extensive training and what was involved in being a close protection specialist and head of the palace security team.

He felt he had talked enough of himself. He was not accustomed to it and was shocked by how easy she was to talk to and how much he had revealed.

"Tell me of your ambitions, then, lass."

She looked tentative. "I've already enjoyed

enormous success, certainly beyond anything I had expected. I mean I've traveled the world, I've met celebrities, I've had a great job and made enormous amounts of money."

"I hear a *but* in there."

"Well, I'm currently unemployed."

"You could have a job like that again in a second if you wanted it."

"I think you're probably right, so I wonder why I'm so hesitant to put my name back out there. I guess I've had what everyone dreams of—the big salary, the traveling, meeting so-called important people. And, I think really, that's the question I've been avoiding. I had it. Why don't I want it again?"

The silence stretched, until finally he had to know.

"Why don't you, Sophie?"

"I don't know."

But he knew she did know. "Tell me."

She cast him a look, then took a deep breath, trusted him with it. "I chaffed at the limitations of Mountain Bend when I lived there, but sometimes I long for the simplicity of that life."

"And yet, within a week of arriving here you told me you were bored," he reminded her.

"*Bored* was probably the wrong term. But *lonely* seemed too pathetic."

"Tell me why you don't want to go back to work in marketing."

"All the glitz and glamour were fun, don't get me wrong, but I felt emptier and emptier. My fiancé seemed to twig to that. He said to me, more than once, *'Your heart isn't in this thing.'* When I think about it now, maybe my heart not being in it was what made him look elsewhere."

"Whatever the problems in your relationship," Connal said sternly, "there is no excuse for him handling them without honor."

"Thank you," she said simply. "When Troy said my heart wasn't in this thing, I guess I thought he meant us, but in retrospect, it was all of it. That lifestyle is a race. You run and run and run. There's no finish line. It doesn't leave any space for—"

She stopped.

"For what?" he prodded her.

"For this. For connection."

"Ah. Tell me about why you said yes to that man, lass." Was he ready to hear? He thought he was.

"He reminded me of someone," she whispered. "That I couldn't have."

He went very still.

"But he was different enough that the intensity was missing. And that intensity—the racing heart and the sweating palms, the thinking about a person night and day—it felt as if I couldn't survive that again. I didn't want to experience that kind of intensity again. The feeling of loss when it didn't work out was like grief that didn't go away."

He stayed very still.

She was talking about *him*, the way she had felt about him.

She was telling him he had broken her heart.

"I felt you nursed illusions about me," he said gruffly, in his own defense.

"I've told myself that over and over," she said softly. "That I was immature. That I was hopelessly infatuated. That night at the christening I told myself that I had had too much to drink."

"You had," he agreed roughly.

"It only unleashed what was already there. My heart has always recognized you, Connal."

He gulped.

"None of my words, none of my rationalizing,

none of my explaining it to myself have made it go away," she confessed softly.

"You know I have nothing to give you," he said. Except maybe that: his absolute honesty. "I'm broken. There is no future with me, lass."

"What if," she whispered softly, "we didn't worry about the future? Or the past? What if we just took what life has given us now? And gave it every bit of heart that we have?"

His own words were coming back to bite him.

She was leaning toward him. And he could not resist. Not this time. With a groan of pure surrender, he tangled his hands in her hair. He pulled what remained of the braid out of her silky locks and combed it with his fingers until it hissed and curled around her head and tumbled over the roundness of her shoulders to the curve of her breast.

There was still time to pull back. If he could just—

Her lips found his.

The kiss reflected everything that Sophie was. It held delicacy and strength, fragility and resilience. They had not eaten strawberries today. Nor had they had wine. And yet, to him, that was what her lips tasted of.

Strawberries. And wine.

And dangerously, and tantalizingly, of the one thing he refused himself.

Hope.

Her lips meeting his held hope.

He reared back from it. And from her. He untangled his hands from her hair, but she caught one, and grazed her lips across it, held it to her cheek.

"I don't think—" he started to say, his voice a growl of pure need, but she never let him finish.

Her finger touched his lips.

"Perfect," she said huskily. "Don't think. Don't think at all."

And just like that the things he was going to say, the things he should have said—*I don't think this is a good idea... I don't think we should do this*—were erased from his mind as though she were an enchantress who had waved her wand.

His chance to pull away was gone as his heart rose toward that thing—that most dangerous thing—that it had waited silently for all these years.

Hope. The opportunity to be alive again. The opportunity for a second chance to get right what he had gotten so very, very wrong his first time around.

He scooped her up in his arms and took her to the bed.

CHAPTER SIXTEEN

IT WAS THIS and only this that she had lived her entire life for, Sophie thought, as Lancaster carried her through the dark cabin, illuminated only by the flickering fire, to the bed. He laid her down across it, tenderly and savagely at the same time. It seemed impossible those two things could exist together, but they did, and their harmony was perfect, shocking, like two flavors that are not supposed to mingle, but did, with amazing results.

He lowered himself over her, holding some of his weight off her with a knee and an elbow. Even then, she could feel the crush of him, the lean hardness of his chest and thigh.

He gazed at her face, and she drank in the strength of his beloved, familiar features. Then with a groan of that same savagery and tenderness, he took her lips.

The tenderness came first, the soft exquisite

exploration, the gentle invitation to open her mouth to his.

And then came the savagery, the plundering of her mouth, the bruising of her lips, the demand that she answer him.

And she did. She answered him with a fury of violent softness, asking, giving, demanding, taking.

This was what she had longed to feel. This was what her heart had known the minute the plane had landed and she had set sight on him again.

That he and he alone could make her feel this way.

Helpless and powerful.

Strong and weak.

She traced the ridges of those braced muscles of his forearms with her fingertips. She felt giddy with the possession of him. Somehow, she managed to get her trembling hands free of the crush of his body, somehow she managed to squeeze her hands between them and find the buttons of his shirt.

She put her hands on both sides, and tore it open with a strength that was shocking and fabulous.

She flattened the palms of her hands against

his chest, as he plundered her mouth. Her ears. Her eyelids. Her neck. Her mouth again.

"I need…" she whispered, then lost her voice, not knowing how to express the enormity of the need.

She needed *more*. She needed to explore every inch of him with her hands and her lips and her tongue. She needed him to explore every inch of her with his hands and his lips and his tongue.

He put his finger to her lips.

"Do you not think I don't know what you need?" he whispered.

Doona.

And then he proved it. He proved he knew exactly what she needed. He had known all along.

Something tickled her nose, and Sophie brushed it away. She never wanted to wake up. She wanted to stay in this world of dreamlike sensation. So safe. So content. So fulfilled.

The tickle again. And then again.

She opened her eyes. Lancaster was standing above her, dressed only in his jeans, tickling her nose with a feather. She drank him in, felt the hunger blossom within her, shut her eyes against it.

He tickled her again.

She opened her eyes. She *wanted* to look at him. She scanned his face and saw such incredible tenderness there she had to bite her lip to keep the tears that sparked behind her eyes from falling.

"I've brought you breakfast," he said. "We have the whole day ahead of us. Let's not waste a second of it."

Carefully balancing the tray, he came into the bed beside her, settling the tray on his thighs. The tray contained steaming coffee, a tin of biscuits and a circle of wildflowers woven with grasses.

Keeping the blanket tucked around her, Sophie struggled to sitting. He handed her a mug of coffee, and then, as she sipped it, he took the circle of flowers and placed it on her head. He regarded her crown with a faint smile, as if bemused at himself.

It was true, some barrier had come down in him, and having it down was beyond her wildest dreams.

"Where did you find flowers at this time of year?" she asked, opening the tin and selecting a biscuit. She took a bite and gave it to him. "Especially after that storm?"

"It's a secret. One I'll share with you after we've had breakfast." He took the biscuit she had handed him, and put his lips exactly where her lips had been. It felt as intimate as anything that had happened between them last night.

After they had polished off the coffee and the tin, she hoped he would just stay in bed, but he leaped up with great energy, took the tray and tossed her clothes at her.

"Come on, lass, the day awaits us." He went out the door.

Moments later, she joined him outside. He had packed a basket full of things, and he took it in the crook of one arm, and extended his hand to her.

She took it, and when their hands joined, just like sharing that biscuit, it felt as momentous as anything that had happened last night. It felt as if they were deeply and joyously connected.

The dew was still on the leaves as they walked through the forest. Lancaster whistled. And then he sang, his rich voice as natural in the forest as the songs of birds.

He sang in a different language, and yet there

was no mistaking, by the tune, that it was a love song, a ballad of the heart, a melody of the soul.

For her.

"Tell me what it means," she begged him.

"You know what it means," he said, and then he threw back his head, laughed and sang more.

The forest path ended in the most beautiful glade she had ever seen. Waterfalls splashed in at the far end of it, and the distinctive scent of hot springs was in the air.

With a whoop of pure joy, Lancaster stripped off to his boxers and ran on nimble feet, scrambling up wet rocks to the top of that falls.

He stood above it and then turned his back to her. He spread his arms, and then lifted himself on his toes. He sprang up and up and up, arched his back and did a full turn, before slicing cleanly into the water.

He surfaced with a shout of laughter, shaking the droplets from his hair. This was Lancaster fully alive.

This was Lancaster in love with life.

And maybe, just maybe, a little bit in love with her.

Showing off for her. Scrambling to the top of that falls again and again, diving, flipping, twisting, plying his amazing strength to the art form of making his body do what he wanted it to do. Sophie went and stood at the edge of the pool he was diving into. She bent and trailed her hand in it. The water was so cold it took her breath away.

Finally, Lancaster's skin pebbled with goose bumps, he left the coldness of the pool. He grabbed some items from the basket and then held out his hand to her. He led her to the hot pool that was nearly hidden under an outcrop in the rocks the waterfall cascaded down.

The same yellow flowers that were in the head-dress he had crowned her with bloomed in glorious abundance around the turquoise waters.

He undid the belt that held her blouse together, and skimmed her slacks off her. He took the ring of flowers from her hair. He led her into the warm water and told her to duck under it.

When she came up, he was lathering soap between his hands. She thought it was for himself and the thought of sharing this pool with him while he bathed nearly made her swoon. But instead of using that abundance of lather on himself, he motioned her to come closer. He began at her head, working the soap deep into her hair, running the tendrils through his soapy hands, scooping water and rinsing. And he worked his way all the way down.

And then, he handed her the soap and turned his back to her.

And so she began on the broadness of his back, working the soap into his hot-springs-warmed skin until it was slick and glorious beneath her fingertips. He stood stock-still while she got to know every inch of him.

And when she was finished, he took her in his arms, and gave her the part of him she had not explored with soap.

His mouth.

He let go into this thing that was unfolding between them, and he let go into it with everything he had, every beat of his heart, every breath that he took. Every look. Every touch.

She let go, surrendering as completely as she had ever surrendered to anything.

The day evaporated as they loved each other. And chased each other. And pushed each other into the cold water, and played along the slippery banks and took long soaks in the hot springs.

The day evaporated as they fed each other small treats of biscuits and tinned oranges and salted almonds from the basket he had packed.

The day evaporated as they sipped cold, pure spring water from the one mug he had brought, and then, dispensing with that, just from each other's cupped hands.

The day evaporated as he wove flowers into her hair, and she massaged the column of his neck, the broadness of his back, the powerful muscles of his shoulders.

The day evaporated as they shared their deepest secrets, their fears and their hopes and their dreams. The day evaporated as their laughter filled the glade and their newly discovered love filled them.

And then the day was, without warning, taken from them.

Sophie saw the second Lancaster heard something. He tilted his head slightly, listening, his eyes narrowed. He had been sitting in the pool beside her, and now, without explanation, he pulled himself from it.

It was a full minute before she heard what he was hearing.

Above the sounds of the water cascading down rocks, above the sounds of birds singing, above the sounds of their laughter and their breath, was a sound that was foreign and seemed like the most violent of intrusions.

She could hear the steady whoop of helicopter blades slicing at the air. At first the sound was faint, but then it grew closer and closer. And as that sound closed in on them, Sophie watched Lancaster change completely. From playful to warrior in the blink of an eye.

"Let's go," he said tersely, holding out his hand to her. She took it and he pulled her from the lovely comfort of the hot water.

The change in his mood was as abrupt as her being yanked from the hot water into the cold air. It was so complete it left her feeling stunned. He quickly toweled off, tossed the towel at her and tugged clothes over his still-wet skin.

He was radiating impatience as he waited for her to do the same. He stepped up to her, and plucked the flowers from her hair. He took the crown he had made her this morning and tossed it in the water below the falls where it floated in an endless, forlorn circle.

He led the way to the trail that led back to the cabin, and went down it fast, two steps ahead of her the whole way, making her struggle to keep up.

Gone was the laughing man who had sung ballads, and dived and played in the water, and put flowers in her hair.

It seemed he was as eager to leave this day behind him as she was to hold on to it forever.

CHAPTER SEVENTEEN

REALITY REARED ITS ugly head as soon as Lancaster heard the helicopters. Those were his men, and they were coming for him.

And for Sophie.

His first thought was that he had to protect her. If his men saw the flowers in her hair, saw any kind of coziness between Lancaster and her, they would jump to those conclusions that men were famous for jumping to.

It was not questions of Lancaster's conduct as a professional that worried him. He did not want what had happened between him and Sophie left open to rough conjecture.

He felt he would probably kill the first man who slid him—or her—a sly look of knowing. Kill the man who clapped him on the back in wordless, brotherly congratulation over his conquest.

This is what he got for letting things slip out of his control. This is what he got for surrendering to the chemistry that had sizzled between them almost from the day they had met.

Spontaneous combustion was not what Sophie deserved.

A tryst in a rustic cabin in the hills was not what she deserved.

How could he have done this to her? She deserved talk of what the future held for them *before* those things that had unfolded between them had unfolded, while they had both been clearheaded. How could they make any clearheaded decisions now? Everything would be clouded, from this day forward, by this day, when they had played like carefree children, but enjoyed the very adult passion that burned white hot between them.

He had gone along with her. Fallen under her enchantment. Live for the moment. No future and no past.

But it was a fantasy. There was a future and there was a past. His past threw shadows forward onto any future she was looking for.

And now both of them were going to have to deal with the consequences of jumping into something without thinking it through.

An awful, awful thought hit him. And yet, the

feeling it gave him was not awful at all. It filled him with the oddest feeling of warmth, even while it increased his need to protect her. They were nearly back at the cabin.

"Is there any chance that you—" He didn't finish the sentence, but he was sure it was crystal clear what he was asking. When his question was met with silence, he stopped and looked back at her.

She had stopped dead in her tracks. She glared at him. If looks could kill a man, he would be six feet under.

"Are you worried about another woman trapping you, Lancaster?"

Lancaster. Not Connal. The change made him feel bereft, even as he could not let her know that.

He was worried about *her*, not himself. He couldn't believe she would throw the history he had trusted her with in his face, but he didn't let the wound show.

"I'm just asking a question," he said, his voice carefully flat.

"Well, if you were so concerned about that, you should have asked it yesterday," she snapped.

Truer words than that had rarely been spoken.

The sound of the helicopters was deafening. They were going to land in the clearing around the cabin.

In Lancaster's world, there was one attribute in a man, or a woman, that mattered more than any other. And that attribute was honor.

And he had just taken hers from her.

Stripped her of her honor by playing around with her as if there was nothing at stake. As if they could just have a day of endless summer together with no consequences. And what did that say of his own honor?

"Sophie," he said, his voice too loud, trying to be heard over the deafening throbbing of the chopper blades, "I'm sorry."

From the look on her face—utter devastation, quickly masked with pride—it occurred to him that somehow, he had stumbled on exactly the wrong thing to say.

Well, it wasn't as if he hadn't warned her he was not exactly a master of sensitivity around women.

But that sounded like an excuse in his own mind, and he despised himself even more for trying to foist any of the responsibility for what had happened onto her. He was 100 percent responsible.

The helicopter landed, and things happened fast. They were on it and airborne within minutes. He was sucked seamlessly back into his world, on a bench seat, trusted comrades on both sides of him, being briefed about the storm devastation on the island and the progress of repairing damage.

He felt a sigh of relief. No one seemed to suspect anything untoward had happened between him and Sophie.

He glanced up at her.

She was sitting on the opposite bench, alone, the seats on either side of her deliberately left empty. Her chin was tilted upward and her face was pale and proud. She did not look toward him.

When he looked at her, he felt the most incredible rush.

It deafened him to whatever the man beside him was saying. It felt as if his whole world was a tunnel that led to her.

He was pretty sure he had never experienced this particular feeling before: longing, hunger, tenderness, protectiveness, desire.

Love.

He recognized it only because he had experienced elements of it once before, in its purest form. With his son.

He stared at her.

It was as if a current passed between them, as if she could sense him looking. She turned and looked back at him, holding his gaze steadily.

It felt as if the breath was leaving his chest.

And with great relief, he knew what to do. He knew how to make this thing right. But was he brave enough to do it?

The helicopter was lowering down to the helipad at the palace. He saw her holding back, waiting for everyone else to disembark. He waited, too.

"Sophie," he said, his voice low, "I have to catch up on some things. But I'll come by and see you tonight."

The look she gave him was withering. "Don't bother," she said, and marched away, her nose in the air.

He watched her go, dumbfounded. And then he found a smile tickling his lips. Nothing with her would ever, ever go quite as he planned it, and for someone who loved control as much as him, how could that be anything but a good thing?

It had been the hardest thing she had ever said! Sophie thought. When he had said he would come see her, she had wanted to collapse against him, scream *yes*, beg him to make it soon.

Because of the need inside her.

The need to be with him in every way a woman could be with a man. Her need to hold him and explore him and know him.

For the first time in her life, she understood need. Real need. Not want. But need like a mother must feel to be with her baby and need like someone starving must have for food, and need like a dying person must have to make all that was wrong right.

But all that need just made her weak when she needed to be strong.

He'd already had one woman who had nearly suffocated him with her neediness. Sophie would not be another!

He had made it clear, by his reaction to the arrival of his men in their clearing, that he regretted every single thing that unfolded between them.

And so even though her need sobbed within

her to beg him, she knew the truth. You could not beg another person to love you.

And you could not go to a man like Lancaster filled with need.

Hadn't he helped her recognize this in herself? That she went for a *type*? That she had an overwhelming need to be protected, to be with someone who made her feel safe in a world that could turn dangerous in the blink of an eye?

She entered the palace.

"I'm so glad you're safe," one of the staff members told her. "You've had a wee adventure, I understand."

A wee adventure.

"The princess wants to see you."

She did not want to see Maddie right now. In this state of exhaustion, her heart in pieces, Maddie of all people would see right through her.

"Could you please tell her I'll see her tomorrow?"

The staff member looked appalled. "Just for a moment? I think she just needs to make sure you're all right."

See? Sophie chided herself. *Self-centered as always. Go let her know you are all right. Without burdening her.*

She entered Maddie's suite and then the bedroom. Maddie was sitting up in bed, reading a book. She glanced up and Sophie stared at her. Her friend, despite being in bed, despite being sick a dozen times a day, looked so darned *well*.

Maddie was radiant. Sophie, thinking about Connal chasing her around the kitchen snapping that towel at her, understood that radiance more than she ever had.

Maddie was a woman who loved and was loved in return.

It made Sophie ache with quiet joy for her friend, and sorrow for herself.

"Are you okay?" Maddie asked. "I heard you were stranded. With Lancaster, which reduced my worry, in one way, and made it worse in another."

"Oh, we were fine," Sophie said breezily.

Maddie looked at her closely. "Oh, Soph."

And at those words, Sophie's attempt at a brave front dissolved. She burst into tears. And flew into her friend's open arms.

"I have to leave," she finally said. "I can't stay here, Maddie. Nothing has changed. No, that is not true. Everything has changed. For the worse."

She stopped just short of confessing that she loved him more than ever, that she felt as if she could die for loving him. She stopped short of confessing the troubling truth that she felt her need to feel protected would eventually suffocate any feelings he had for her.

How could she risk running into him now? How could she ever look at him again, without feeling his hands on her, his lips branding her, without thinking of the way his head tilted when he laughed, or the way sweat gilded his muscles when he cut wood?

She could not share a world with him. It was that simple. And that hard.

"What happened?" Maddie asked, wide-eyed.

She couldn't tell her the whole truth. "Things just got out of hand," she fudged uneasily.

"Out of hand? Like *that* out of hand? Lancaster?" Maddie asked, incredulous that Lancaster had lost his legendary self-control.

"It's just more of the same, Maddie," Sophie said sadly. "I'm wild for him, and I think he finds it all just an amusement at best, and an embarrassment at worst. The idea that his men might figure out something had happened between us mortified him."

"Something happened between you?" Maddie asked. "Like *that* happened between you?"

"Maddie, please. I'm not a child. He certainly isn't a child. We're two consenting adults, and we…er…consented. But I can't be running into him, fearing running into him. I can't stay here one more day. Maybe not even one more hour."

Other people, other friends, might have encouraged her to wait, to take a breath, to think things through. But Maddie, thankfully, understood immediately and completely. And Maddie was one of the few people on this island with the power to get things done fast. She could order up a plane.

"I'll arrange it right away," Maddie said. "Come back in an hour and I'll have all the details for you."

"Thank you, Maddie."

"I remember what it is to leave this island with a broken heart, Sophie."

Only you got a happy ending, Sophie thought.

But when she came back in an hour, both Edward and Maddie were there. Edward did most of the talking.

"There's a threat against me?" Sophie asked, skeptically. "That's ridiculous."

Except, when he explained it to her, it wasn't ridiculous. It had a kind of diabolical brilliance to it.

Still, Sophie felt lied to in every possible way. She had been brought to Havenhurst under a pretext of helping her friend.

Lancaster had *known* she was being lied to. He might have even instigated the lie. For her own good, of course, because he knew what was good for everyone. All. The. Time.

The awareness of the threat made Sophie feel that feeling that had been a part of her since the attack on her mother.

The world was not safe. It was scary. Unpredictable and bad things could happen.

But, in that awareness, something brand-new occurred to her.

She had to be able to rely on herself. She had to trust that somewhere in her she had the courage, the instinct, the heart to protect herself from the danger that was inherent to living life. She had continually looked outside herself. To a man. Now, suddenly, it seemed imperative that she find her own bravery.

She did not want to cause Maddie any undue stress. But how could her staying also not cause stress? With such raw divisions in the household? With tension between her and Lancaster palpable in the air?

And one thing she was not going to do? Stay here trapped in a bunch of lies. Of course, there was no way to get on—or off—this island without Lancaster knowing. That's why she was here. Because he was in control of everything. Not that he'd had the decency to tell her that.

Even though there had been lots of opportunities. Never once in the past few days, as they had bared their souls—and an unfortunate amount of other things, too—to each other, had he said, *Lass, there is something I must tell you.*

There was no escaping from Havenhurst. Except Maddie had done it once. Sophie wondered if she could ask her how. But suddenly she knew.

When you were in trouble, there was a certain kind of man you could call. The kind of man she had always been drawn to.

Lancaster was one of them, but he was out of the question.

The other one was her Uncle Kettle.

And that would solve two problems with one stone. Because if Maddie knew she was with Kettle, she would not worry about her either.

After she got free of Havenhurst, then Sophie would uncover her own brave heart. She swore it, a vow to herself.

CHAPTER EIGHTEEN

CONNAL FELT LIKE an idiot. He should have thought of the sideways looks he would be garnering, walking through the palace with a bouquet of flowers.

Not just any bouquet. No, he'd had to ask for a large one. At the time, he hadn't given a thought to the fact it would make it hard to tuck it inside a bag or behind his back. Now he had to endure *these* looks, the knowing smiles from the women, the winks from the men.

He passed a trash can and forced himself not to ditch the bouquet. He was braver than that, wasn't he?

Lancaster had made a vow to himself, and it began with this bouquet.

He would do it right this time. In a way, maybe he was being given a chance to make up for all the times in his life he had done it so wrong.

Been so insensitive, and so self-centered.

A jerk. He had been a total jerk.

But this time, what if he brought flowers, big embarrassing bouquets that made the whole palace whisper about a romance? What if he wrote poetry in the rich language of his ancestors, and translated it for her? What if he packed picnics and they took long walks? What if he took her on ordinary dates, to the movies, to the pub, to *ceilidhs*? What if he wooed her slowly, swept her off her feet, treated her with the honor that she deserved?

What if he backtracked so that the horse went before the cart?

He arrived at the door to Sophie's suite within the palace. He was a man who had exited helicopters on ropes, rappelled down the sides of mountains, jumped out of airplanes. He was a man who had dived off the tops of cliffs into pools so small they had looked like teacups way down below him. He could not possibly be afraid to be bringing flowers to a woman.

The racing of his heart said differently. He took a deep breath. And he knocked.

There was no answer.

He knocked again, and again. He frowned. She might be at the nursery or with Maddie. But in an hour, he knew Sophie was in none of those places. He went back to her room, knocked again and opened the door.

He could *sense* the emptiness, even before he went and flung open the closet doors. Her clothes were gone. The chest of drawers was empty. Even the bathroom had been swept clean. Only a bottle of shampoo remained, on the ledge of the tub. He resisted the urge to go and smell it, to fill his senses with something beyond the emptiness that was moving through him like winter ice claiming a lake.

He went back into the main room and saw an envelope on her bed.

It was addressed to Connal, not Lancaster, and that gave him the tiniest hope. Funny how not so long ago it had been the opposite. He had not wanted her to use his first name. Now he did not want to lose that small intimacy between them.

He opened the envelope and fished a single piece of paper from it.

It was so nice to have a chance to see you let down your guard! I've had an opportunity come up that I can't say no to, but if I ever get stranded in the wilderness again I hope it's with you.

Don't forget to have some fun from time to time, Connal.
Sophie

P.S. It might have been nice if you'd let me know there was a plot with my name on it, but don't worry about me. Read The Ransom of Red Chief!

It was everything he could do not to tear the note to shreds and fill that room with a howl of pure rage and frustration. She could, at this very moment, be walking blithely into danger. And she was dismissing it, writing polite little thank-you notes of the kind that one might give to a great aunt who had invited you to tea.

"Who the hell is Red Chief?" he asked, moments later of Prince Edward. He tossed the note down on the prince's desk.

In this moment, he felt his deep kinship with the prince, the barriers of station between them removed by years of the friendship that had made them like brothers.

Edward scanned the note. Surely he wasn't smiling? This was serious business. Sophie had managed to give them the slip and could be in mortal danger. But that did seem to be a small smile tickling Edward's lips.

"She's not in any danger, Lancaster—*Connal*—I'm sure of that."

"Do you know where she is, then? Has she confided in Maddie?"

"I don't know exactly where she is, and as far as I know, she hasn't said anything to Maddie. But we've been through this once before. Surely you have not forgotten Maddie's escape from Havenhurst?"

Lancaster took a deep breath. Kettle. Sophie would have called Kettle.

Still. "It's not funny, sir."

"Well, the reference to *The Ransom of Red Chief* is. Not familiar with that story, Lancaster?"

He shook his head.

"It's about a group of thugs who kidnap the child of extremely wealthy parents. By the end of his stay with them they are negotiating how much they will pay to give him back."

"She is a handful," Lancaster said with resignation.

"And she's your handful, isn't she, Lancaster?" his friend asked him with soft sympathy and grave affection. With a *knowing* of Lancaster's heart that only a brother could have.

"I'm afraid she is that, sir."

"Then go and use all those skills you've been acquiring your whole life—maybe in preparation for this very moment—and get her."

For the first time, ever so reluctantly, Lancaster smiled, too. "I will."

Sophie heard something outside, and she jumped, then strained her ears, listening. She was embarrassed by how nervous she was, possibly worse than she had ever been.

On the other hand, she had been educating herself rigorously on the topic of fear. According to what she was learning, sometimes fear could be a gift. For instance, she *was* the target of a kidnapping plot. Her fear gave her an opportunity to address that reality, to prepare, to not be a helpless victim in the face of a threat.

She forced herself to do as the online course on fear suggested. She drew in a deep breath, allowed herself to feel it fill her lungs, let it out. It clarified her thinking almost instantly.

Really, the past few days had felt like something out of a cloak-and-dagger book.

Kettle, enlisting several of his old navy SEAL friends, had whisked her away from Havenhurst with ease. He had grumbled a bit about Maddie—and now her—pulling him out of retirement, but she could tell he quite enjoyed the rescue.

She had not told Kettle, though, the part about the kidnap plot, because she was pretty sure he would have left her to Lancaster's care had he known about it.

No one trusted her to be that person who could look after themselves.

There was a knock on the door and Sophie nearly jumped out of her skin.

Again, she forced calm on herself, took a deep breath. She was pretty sure a kidnapper would not lose the element of surprise by knocking on the door. Still, her heart was beating way too fast.

In her mind, she reviewed the self-defense moves she had been teaching herself, also via an online course. She checked the location of the baseball bat, behind the door, and then she crept to the front window to peer out.

She could see someone very large on the front

porch of the little house Kettle had put her in in Cannon Beach.

"No one will find you here until you are good and ready to be found," he'd assured her. Kettle being Kettle, thankfully he had not asked her for any of the details leading up to her mad dash from Havenhurst.

The fear in her stood down. Sophie knew it was Lancaster. It wasn't just the size of the shadow out there, it was that deep sense of *knowing*.

The fear was replaced by outrage. Of course he would arrive to claim her back! She had slipped his control. It was his job to protect her from some shadowy threat, and he would not like it one bit that she had thwarted that.

"Open the door, Sophie."

The voice alone was enough to melt her resolve not to be his job, not to be protected by him, not to need him in any way.

"No," she said.

"Don't make me kick it down."

A little shiver went up and down her spine. Good grief. He was being primitive. That shiver wasn't a shiver of pure, well...thrill, was it?

"I know how to defend myself."

"As if you have to defend yourself against me."

"You're the one who threatened to kick down the door."

"Sophie, please be reasonable. Open the door."

As always, just a little too sure of his ability to convince her. There was that little thrill again. There was no point in his knowing what kind of power he wielded over her. That was the message hiding behind a locked door would give him.

Taking a deep breath, she moved to the door and threw it open.

He stood there, so beautiful and so beloved to her that she wanted to touch the now oh-so-familiar plains of his face.

She glanced down the full length of him, and then back up into his face. There was something there. He looked worn out, haggard.

"You're wearing a kilt," she pointed out to him.

"Aye," he said.

"But you told me you only wear it for special occasions."

"Aye," he said again.

"Oh! Bringing the escapee from your protection back into custody is a special occasion?"

"They apprehended everyone in the ring two days ago. The danger to you is over."

"That's too bad. I'm learning self-defense. I was hoping for an opportunity to use it."

"I hope you're kidding."

"About learning self-defense?"

"About being in danger so you have an opportunity to practice."

Really? The way her heart was beating it felt as if she was in more danger than she had ever been in in her entire life.

"Then you just dropped by on your way back from accompanying the prince to a state dinner or something?"

"You know as well as I do the prince would not leave his princess right now."

Faint recrimination there? Because she had left her friend?

"I had to go," she said firmly. "How did you find out where I am? What have you done with my uncle? He would have never given my whereabouts away willingly."

"He did. Willingly."

Her heart dropped to the bottom of her stomach. "Is something wrong? Did something happen to Maddie? Or the baby? Is that why Edward won't leave her right now? Is that why Kettle told you where I was?"

But that didn't make sense. Kettle could have come and told her himself if something was wrong with Maddie.

"Everyone's fine," he said softly. "Except…" His voice trailed away.

"Except who?" she implored him.

"Isn't it obvious who?" he asked her softly.

She looked, again, at the weariness in his face, the haggardness.

"It's you," she said, and then even though she did not want to, she reached up and cupped his cheek in the palm of her hand. She felt him surrender into that touch.

"Aye, lass, it's me. Are you going to leave me standing on the stoop all night?"

She stepped back from the door, and he walked by her, the heavy kilt swirling around his legs. It was enough to make a girl swoon!

"Have a seat," she said to him, with a little more snap than was strictly necessary.

He did, and she took a chair at right angles to him.

Do not look at his knees, she ordered herself.

"What's wrong, Lancaster?"

"I need to talk to you about those days at the cabin," he said.

"Could we not?" she said. "Please? I totally got it when you were embarrassed by it in front of your men. I got it, Lancaster. I'm a slow learner but I finally figured it out. I'm needy. The thing you hate the most. It was probably more than evident after those days together that I would need you. The way a flower needs rain. Or a puppy needs love. Or a—"

He was staring at her, stunned. "You thought I was embarrassed about you?"

"Oh, sure. I understand it. Crazy American woman fawning over you in front of people. I mean it's one thing to chase each other around in privacy, quite another to be chased when you have a reputation to uphold. When I was supposed to be your—what word do you guys use?—*principal*, and you broke the cardinal rule. You let it get personal. I can see that—"

"Be quiet," he growled. "I can't listen to one more second of this. You have it so wrong. So utterly and completely wrong. You are hurting my ears."

"I have it wrong?"

I'm hurting your ears? The nerve! But something in his tormented features saved her from anger.

"I wasn't embarrassed by you," he said softly. "Not ever. I was embarrassed by myself. By my total loss of control."

"Oh," she said, folding her arms over her chest, "you have no idea how much better that makes me feel. That's sarcasm, in case you missed it."

"I took your honor," he said, his voice low. "I compromised my own. That's what I didn't want my men to see. I didn't want them drawing conclusions about you. About us."

"Well, good, you seemed to have handled all that quite nicely. I feel I left Havenhurst with my reputation intact, and I have you to thank for that. I'm also learning to protect myself. Because I'm not ever going to rely on someone else to do that for me again."

He glowered at her. "A man likes to protect a woman."

"Too bad."

He groaned. "Why are you making this so difficult?"

"*I'm* making things difficult? I didn't show up on your doorstep in a sexy outfit. You showed up on mine. What is the occasion by the way? For the kilt?"

"You're wrecking everything," he said.

"I'm not."

"I wore the kilt for the most special occasion of my entire life." His voice went very low, a rasp. "I wore it to propose to you."

She went very still. "Wh-what?"

"To propose. To ask you to marry me."

"That seems to be going a little far just to protect my reputation. And your honor."

"Do you have to be so bloody pigheaded! I'm not proposing to you because I want to protect your reputation. Or my honor. I'm proposing to you because I got it so wrong, chasing you around the cabin, treating you without respect. Something like this needs to be treated with respect."

"Something like what?"

"Something like me falling in love with you. Something like you falling in love with me. That's what really happened at the cabin."

It felt as if a light was coming on in darkness. "That happened way, way before the cabin, Connal."

"For me, too," he admitted. "Probably from the first time I laid eyes on you and told myself, this is a lass I cannot have."

Canna.

"I'm just afraid," he said, his voice hoarse.

This man, who seemed so fearless, laying his most vulnerable possession before her. Showing her his heart and his deepest fear. Finally, finally, finally, laying down his shield and his sword.

"I'm afraid. Afraid that I failed so badly once before, and that I will fail again. That's why I want to start over. That's why I want to court you. I want to romance you, and cherish you, and take every step slowly, making sure I am moving in the right direction. That *we* are moving in the right direction."

"I hope you aren't planning on being completely chaste about this," Sophie said. The lightness in her heart made it impossible not to tease him when he was being so darned serious, so intense.

His eyes darkened as he looked at her lips. "Maybe not completely."

Then she could not wait any longer. She flew to him, into the arms that opened and then closed around her. She covered his face in kisses.

"Can I take that as a yes?" he said.

"Yes."

"Then get off of me. I have to make it official."

She left his lap and watched as he slid to the

floor, and on one bended knee—making his kilt ride up enticingly—fished around for a ring box, found it, opened it.

"Sophie Kettle, will you marry me?"

It felt as though the stars winked on, one by one, against a dark night. It felt as if she was a balloon that had been deflated and now found air. It felt as if a world that had been black and white went to full color.

"Yes," she whispered.

And he whooped and found his feet and gathered her in his arms and swung her around and around and around until the world was a rainbow swirl of nothing but love.

* * * * *

LET'S TALK

Romance

For exclusive extracts, competitions
and special offers, find us online:

f facebook.com/millsandboon

⊙ @millsandboonuk

🐦 @millsandboon

Or get in touch on 0844 844 1351*

For all the latest titles coming soon,
visit millsandboon.co.uk/nextmonth